ULTIMATE CURVES

A collection of twenty erotic stories

Edited by Miranda Forbes

Published by Accent Press Ltd – 2009
ISBN 9781906373788

Copyright © Accent Press Ltd 2009

The stories contained within this book are works of fiction. Names and characters are the products of the authors' imagination and any resemblance to actual persons, living or dead, is entirely coincidental.

All rights reserved. No part of this book may be reproduced, stored in a retrieval system, or transmitted in any form or by any means, electronic, electrostatic, magnetic tape, mechanical, photocopying, recording or otherwise, without the written permission of the publishers: Accent Press Ltd, The Old School, Upper High St, Bedlinog, Mid-Glamorgan, CF46 6RY

Printed in the UK by CPI Bookmarque, Croydon, CR0 4TD

Cover Design by
Red Dot Design

Contents

The Watcher	Kristina Wright	1
Clara's Cakes	Izzy French	8
Private Dancer	Carole Archer	19
Love at First Light	Harriet Hamblin	28
Princess Beatrice	Sadie Wolf	39
Where Phone Sex Can Lead	Deva Shore	51
Wanted, Exhibitionists	Jennie Treverton	62
In the Bakery	Kristina Wright	76
Watching	Victoria Blisse	85
The Photographer's Muse	Scarlett Sanderson	97
Meeting My Husband Again	Deva Shore	106
Fashionably Late	Heidi Champa	116
A Lucky Man	Lucy Felthouse	123
The Beautiful Move in Curves	Elizabeth Black	130
Chocolate Lover	Victoria Blisse	143
Mama Nana	Alcamia	152
Two for One	Kitti Bernetti	162
Workout	Beverly Langland	169
Painted Lady	Amelia Fox	179
The Ivory Tower	Izzy French	187

New! Ultimate Curves for sexy, curvy, lovable ladies…

A place for sexy, curvy girls and the men who love them!

Sexy, Curvy, Gorgeous!

ULTIMATE curves

Join today!
Quality dating   Free erotic stories   Plus size lingerie
www.ultimatecurves.com

Quality dating, free stories and plus-size lingerie

www.ultimatecurves.com

The Watcher
by Kristina Wright

He was watching her again. Maisy smiled as she walked across her bedroom, naked and still damp from the shower. The smell of lilacs filled the softly lit room. She was alone tonight. Her roommates were gone for the evening and she had the place to herself. She intended to give her watcher an evening to remember.

Standing in front of the open window, she shivered as a light breeze dried the water from her pale skin. She looked upward, toward the night sky, not at the man across the street who sat in his own bedroom watching her. Stretching her arms over her head, she pulled her long blonde hair up and away from her neck. She arched her back toward the window, catching a glimpse of herself in the mirror in the corner of the room. She looked like a woman waiting for a lover. Tonight, the stranger who watched her was her lover and her body was for his pleasure.

For a long time, Maisy had thought the watcher was watching her roommates. Sara and Karen were thin, lithe little things who made men's heads turn on the street. Sara even modelled occasionally, for goodness sake! The three women had speculated about the watcher over the past couple of months, debating whether they should do anything about him. Sara and Karen breezily accepted the idea that he was, in fact, watching them. They were used to the attention. But it had caught Maisy quite by surprise to find the watcher in his usual spot on several occasions when neither of her roommates was around. And it wasn't as if he was waiting for them, either. In fact, she found herself watching the watcher and noting how quickly he abandoned his post when Sara or Karen arrived home.

It thrilled her to know he was watching her.

Dusk had fallen and she knew she was backlit in the window, erotically framed in the brackets of her red curtains like a Rubens painting for his private viewing. She fleetingly wondered if anyone else might be watching her from the darkened buildings, but it didn't matter. The watcher across the way – her watcher – was the only one she was interested in. She could see him sitting in his usual chair facing the window. It was hard to tell what he looked like and she didn't have the nerve to use binoculars to study him, but she could tell his shoulders were broad and his hair was dark. She imagined he was older than her, an older man with a penchant for women with soft curves and plump bottoms. He was a shadowy figure in a darkened room, watching her. Appreciating her. Desiring her.

"Go on, then," she whispered to him. "Get a good look at me."

She let her hair cascade through her fingers as she dropped her hands to her shoulders. She gently kneaded and soothed the muscles of her neck and shoulders like an imaginary lover. As if he was impatient for her to get on with it, the watcher shifted in his chair. He wore a white shirt and dark pants. Fully clothed in comparison to her brazen nudity. She had never seen him do more than watch and now she found herself aroused at the thought of seeing him naked.

"Want more, do you?" she giggled. "Well, let's give you more."

With that, she cupped her plump breasts in her hands, the soft flesh spilling over her fingers. She closed her eyes and imagined it was him touching her. Her nipples tightened under her fingertips, becoming hard, pink pebbles aching to be touched and sucked. A soft moan escaped her as she tugged gently on them and felt a corresponding tingle of sensation between her thighs. The sounds of the evening traffic fell away and all she could hear were her own little whimpers of desire.

Her eyes fluttered open and she saw the watcher leaning forward. Anxious. As anxious as she was, she imagined. She felt nervous with anticipation, as if waiting for her lover to fuck her. She stared at him and mouthed the words, "I want you."

He didn't seem to notice. Or, if he did, he didn't know what to make of it. What was she hoping for? That he would leave his post at the window and rush over to her bedroom? For a total stranger to toss her down on her bed and fuck her silly?

Yes, that was exactly what she wanted. She said it again, out loud, even though there was no way he could hear her. "I want you."

Maisy ran her hands down to her stomach, stroking the soft curve of her belly, teasing herself as much as she was teasing him. Her skin felt warm, tingly. She slipped her hand between her thighs, caressing the silky blonde tuft of hair on her fleshy mound. The watcher stared, still as a statue, as she slipped a finger into her pussy. She gasped at how wet she was already. Wet and hot, the dull throb between her thighs was building to a sharp ache of need.

In anticipation for this evening, she had dragged an armchair from the living room into her bedroom and positioned it in front of the window. She sat now, her knees a bit wobbly from her excitement, and propped her feet on the windowsill. Her hand was still between her thighs, but she pressed her knees together to hide herself from his view. She wanted to see what – if anything – he might do.

He sat there for a moment, watching. Waiting. When she didn't spread her legs, he stood up and walked closer to the window. He looked tall. Muscular. Formidable. A shaft of light from the streetlight fell across his face, illuminating his intense expression. He looked like a man possessed, all of his attention focused on one thing. Her.

She caught her breath.

His lips moved, saying something. She strained to make out the words. He said it again. This time she understood what he was saying. Her pulse pounded in her ears as the watcher suddenly became a participant in her exhibitionism.

"Spread your legs," he was telling her.

She let her knees fall open. He nodded in approval.

Maisy fondled her pussy while he watched, dipping her fingers into her wetness and dragging her damp fingertips over her swollen clit. She slid down in the chair so that her bottom was at the edge of the cushion, her pussy pushed toward him. She braced her feet on either side of the window, spread wide for him. A wet, succulent offering for her watcher.

He was still standing at his window, nodding. She watched as his hand dropped to his crotch and he rubbed himself. Her pussy rippled in response to this overt sign of his arousal. She longed for him to unzip his pants and reveal his erection, to show her what she had only imagined. He didn't go that far, however. He just stood there, watching her and rubbing himself through his trousers.

Parting the engorged lips of her slit with one hand, Maisy pushed two fingers deep inside her dripping pussy. She moaned as she stroked herself, showing him how he could fuck her, if only he were here. She could almost feel his gaze like a touch between her legs while she fucked herself for him. She worked her fingers inside her pussy, trying to quench the ache deep inside, her pussy making obscene wet, slurping sounds as she stroked herself. Her cheeks flushed with embarrassment, as if her watcher could actually hear the unladylike sounds her body was making.

"Fuck me," she whimpered, pleading with a man who could not hear her. "Please."

She looked at him, thrusting her hips up to meet her fingers as if it was his cock she was fucking. He put a hand on the window, his fingers splayed like he was reaching out to touch her but the glass had stopped him. She moaned loudly, wondering if the sound might carry across the street. God, how she wanted him here, the watcher fucking her instead of only watching her touch herself. He was feeding her desire, pushing her higher. It wasn't about putting on a show for him any longer – it was about her passion, her excitement.

Her need for release was building to an unbearable ache. She had intended to tease him all night, stroking and fondling herself to show him what he was missing. But now all she could think about was her orgasm. She wanted to come, was so close to it already that she knew it wouldn't take but a few more strokes to send her into a spiralling climax. There would be more where that came from, of course, but would he keep watching? Would he decide to close the curtains and leave her then? Or would he stay with her, mesmerised by the way she touched herself, made herself come?

She could barely think any longer. She felt flush with fever, her skin damp with sweat. Her body hummed with her desire, her muscles quivering with the need for release. She clenched her pussy around her fingers, feeling the first tremors of orgasm building low in her belly. Her plump thighs trembled as she rocked back and forth on her fingers. She watched him mimic her motions with the sway of his own narrow hips, whether consciously or unconsciously she had no way of knowing. But it was all it took to push her over the edge, to drive her to the exquisite release her body longed for so desperately.

She screamed out her release, her cries of pleasure echoing off the walls of her bedroom and seeming to fill the night with her voice. The intensity of her orgasm was too powerful to focus on the watcher any longer. She closed her eyes tightly but his silhouette was burned into her memory, a dark vision behind her eyelids, watching her fuck herself. Watching her come. She thrust against her fingers as if they were his cock, wringing every last sensation from her overwrought body.

Her orgasm seemed to go on for ever. Just as one ripple faded away, another would slam into her, dragging her down under a wave of pleasure so intense it left her panting. There wasn't a coherent thought in her head, only this unrelenting need that she could not seem to satiate.

Finally, slowly, the spirals of desire began to fade. Her pussy still rippled around her fingers, but the intense ache of need had shifted to a feeling of languid satisfaction. She was still breathing hard, her body as damp as if she had just left the shower. She kept stroking herself, moving her fingers inside her, feeling the tingle of response that let her know it wouldn't take much to build back to the same intensity of a few moments ago. She dropped her feet to the floor, feeling the muscles in her calves and thighs protest. She ached as if she had been well and truly fucked and, in her own mind, she had. Suddenly, remembering the watcher, she opened her eyes.

He was gone. His window was dark and empty, as if he was an apparition who had vanished with her orgasm.

She sat up, peering across the darkness, looking for some sign of him. She felt empty, bereft at his abandonment. She shivered, her damp skin feeling suddenly cool in the night air that ruffled the curtains. Slumping back in the chair, she sighed with a strange combination of disappointment and anger. Without her watcher, she felt no need to coax her body into another frenzy of desire. His enthusiastic voyeurism made her hot but without it she felt rather silly sitting in an open window.

She stood up and slammed the window closed, hearing it echo hollowly. She went still, listening carefully. Then she heard it again. Not an echo. A knock at her door.

Maisy took a deep, steadying breath as she slipped into her dressing gown. Then she went to the door and let the watcher in.

Clara's Cakes
by Izzy French

Clara stood in the middle of her studio, eyes tight shut. She smoothed her skirt and apron over her ample hips. This was the moment of truth. She wished she had a great big strip of sumptuous red satin ribbon and a huge pair of scissors. Then she could do her very own proverbial grand opening. But instead, 'Clara's Cakes' would open with a whimper rather than a bang. In a moment she'd have to open her eyes, step forward and begin cooking. Her first order for some fancy schmancy cupcakes for a posh patisserie in St John's Wood was due to be collected at noon. Along with forty éclairs for a deli in Soho. So, eyes wide open, she took a deep breath and stepped forward to the sparklingly clean counter.

An hour or so later she was delighted to be able to stand back, pull her apron over her head and admire her handiwork. Sixty perfect morsels of fluffy lightness embellished with icing in a range of soft pastel colours and silver balls were ready to be packed into a box. Next to them were six rows of small but perfectly formed chocolate éclairs. She still had to fill them with crème anglaise. She glanced at the clock. There was time, yet. She picked up a flat-packed box and began to open it up and slot the flaps into place.

"Hey, got a parcel for Patisserie Chocolat?"

Clara was startled at the deeply masculine voice and leather-clad figure standing in front of her. She hadn't heard him come in. Obviously the buzzer system wasn't working. She'd need to get that checked out.

"Those look good enough to eat."

"Corny line. And don't think that'll get you one. They're all spoken for."

"I wasn't talking about the cakes. I'm Joel."

His eyes were firmly fixed on her breasts. She glanced down. She'd worked hard physically for the last hour. Her dress had pulled apart slightly across her chest, she could see the black lace that edged her bra and some small nuggets of icing nestled in her cleavage. No doubt her round cheeks would be glowing, and she suspected there would also be telltale traces of molten chocolate around her lips. Her hair felt like it had worked itself loose from her severe ponytail, and she tried to blow strands of it away from her cheek. There was a good reason she cooked for a living. She had a sweet tooth, a fussy palate and the hips, thighs, rounded stomach and breasts to show for it.

Clara blushed. She'd tried to dress carefully this morning. Although she was working alone, she didn't want to fall into sloppy habits straightaway. So she'd taken her designer wraparound jersey dress from the wardrobe and pulled it tightly over her best black satin bra. She'd finished off with a little twirl in front of the mirror. Her dress fanned round her hips, complementing her curves perfectly, and her heels showed off her calves, knees and thighs to their best advantage. She wasn't worried about marking her dress; it would be well covered by her brand new chef's apron.

He was pulling his motorcycle helmet off now. Did he think he was staying? Clara watched him in silence. He was gorgeous. She'd always gone for the blond Aussie, surfer-dude type. And here was the perfect example of the species standing before her. He shook his shoulder-length hair. She gulped, and couldn't stop herself licking her lips. But they'd never gone for her. Not till now. They always seemed to go for women who looked just like them. Athletic, tanned. Blonde hair down to their pert little arses. Not plump, pale-skinned brunettes.

"You'll need to hang around for a moment or two. The cakes aren't boxed up yet."

"No worries. I can wait."

He hoisted himself on to the counter.

"You can't sit there. There are rules. Regulations. Food hygiene. Health and safety."

"Fuck health and safety," he said.

"And then there are the copious amounts of icing sugar that will now be dusting your arse."

He glanced down at the counter. Then he ran his fingers through the white dust. He grinned and drew two big circles. She thought he was drawing breasts. Her breasts by the size and shape of them. Then he added two nipples in their centres. That confirmed it.

"Do men ever grow up? You're the same the world over. Boys for ever, despite outward appearances to the contrary."

She was trying to use her very best prim and proper English rose voice. But it wasn't working. It came out as a bit of a squeak. He jumped down from the counter and brushed the white powder from his arse.

"Nah, 'course we don't."

He walked over to where she'd half finished packing the box. He stood so close she could feel the warmth of his breath on her cheek.

"Think you've missed a bit."

He touched her cheek, scooping a smudge of chocolate up on his finger, licking it slowly, rubbing it across his lips.

"Buttercream. My favourite."

"You're an expert then?"

He nodded.

"Trained as a chef over in Oz. Couldn't get work here. Thus the couriering. Still if I get to meet gorgeous women like you, and taste their wares, then it's worth the sacrifice."

"I don't recall offering you a taste of my wares." Clara attempted to sound huffy. He obviously wasn't convinced. The next thing she knew his hands were cupping her face, and his lips were on hers, sweet and moist. He kissed her lightly at first, and she found it impossible not to respond to him as he dropped his hands, encircling her more than tiny waist. Then he pushed her lips apart with his tongue. This felt electric, and she couldn't resist entangling her tongue around his, each of them taking turns to explore the other's mouth. Finally he pulled away. Her lips were tingling, as were other parts of her body. She gritted her teeth, closed her eyes tight shut again, hoping against hope that he wasn't going to leave her now. Pick up the box, and walk out of the door.

"You're beautiful," he whispered, reaching around the back of the dress, pulling on her carefully tied bow. Her dress fell apart, revealing her underwear. He raised his eyebrows. She thrust her right hip forward, wondering what he was going to say. Or do.

"I wasn't expecting that," was all he could manage.

"What?" she questioned, attempting to sound innocent, knowing that under the demure but shapely dress, her underwear was sexy, provocative. Her full breasts spilled over her black lace bra. She wore a matching garter belt and stockings. And nothing else. Her hips and thighs looked pale against the black satin and silk. Her pussy was smooth. Nominally, this was to keep her cool, but she knew it was for far more than that. Her garter belt rested just below her waist, emphasising the roundness of her belly. No doubt, for modesty's sake, she should have covered herself, reached for her apron or placed her hand across her pussy, at least. But she didn't. He gulped. She saw Joel's Adam's apple bob in his throat.

"Like it?" She did a shimmy, her breasts moved from side to side, despite the firm hold of her bra, her thighs and stomach rippled.

He nodded. She'd rendered him speechless, apparently.

"How about this?"

She turned around, leant on the counter and bent over. Again she gave a shimmy, a shake of her arse. Out of the corner of her eye she saw him make a move. He picked something up. The next thing she felt was a sharp sting on her arse cheeks. And she saw pale green buttercream icing fly in an arc across the studio.

"Ouch," she protested. A bit.

The spoon slapped her again. And again. She squirmed, sticking her arse out further, inviting him to slap her even more. This felt good. What the kiss had started, this continued, and the tingle that had begun in her lips radiated throughout her body, concentrating, of course, between the lips of her shaven pussy. Not that he wouldn't be fully aware of that. She held tightly on to the edge of the counter, dropping her head, stepping her legs apart slightly, giving him a view of her arsehole, her shaven cunt. He placed the spoon on the counter and bent to touch his tongue to her arse cheeks, licking up the spots of buttercream with the tip of his tongue, making tiny circles at first, covering more of her dimpled flesh as he devoured the icing. And her arse.

"This tastes good," he sighed. And she was quite certain her didn't mean just the icing as he knelt and buried his face between her buttocks, lapping at her cunt, grasping her arse with his hands, sucking up the juices that flowed from her. He licked down the length of each of her outer lips. Then she felt his tongue dart around inside her, and, no doubt, he could feel her cunt tense around it. She ground herself back down on to him, loving the feeling.

Moments later she felt him pull away. She couldn't suppress her feeling of disappointment.

"No, please, more." He grabbed her waist, and turned her around, grinning at her.

"Of course, but I think I'm at a bit of a disadvantage. He pulled his boots off then unbuttoned his leather trousers, and, with some help from Clara, eased them to the floor.

"I like a snug fit," she whispered.

Then he unzipped his jacket, threw it to the corner of the kitchen, shortly followed by his tight-fitting T-shirt. His erection pushed away at his boxers, threatening to escape. They caught each other's eye.

"What the hell," he said, stepping out of them and releasing his cock, which bounced in front of him. Clara was desperate to get her hands on it. To get her lips around it, in fact, and practise a bit of deep throat. But Joel appeared to have other ideas. He'd spotted the bain-marie on the hob. The gas was still on low underneath a glass bowl a quarter full of melted dark chocolate.

"Be a shame to waste it?"

She smiled. He lifted her on to the counter. She spread her legs apart, shuffled her arse forward, leaning back on her palms, anticipating his next move. He reached for a spatula amongst the many kitchen implements she kept in containers on the countertop, then scooped a generous amount of the chocolate from the bain-marie, dashing back to her, his cock bobbing, chocolate dripping from the spatula. Clara drew breath as he smeared the chocolate over her shaven pussy in a careful triangle.

"Good with, good without," he smiled. It was hot but bearable. He went back for another spatula full. This time he smeared it over her inner thighs. The third spatula was destined to insinuate its way into her folds. Clara decided there was nothing quite like the feeling of warm chocolate being spread over her clit. She threw her head back and groaned, shaking her tits, her nipples almost working free from her bra. Then she felt his tongue. First on her thighs. Then on her shaven mound, devouring her and the chocolate in equal parts. Then he pushed her thighs apart and delved into her lips and cunt, from the front this time. He darted over her clit, sending quivers of excitement shooting through her. He explored each and every fold, before encircling her cunt opening, then plunging deep inside her. His fingers slipped over her clit; he'd left some chocolate behind, obviously. She knew she was about to lose control, knowing he was tasting a special blend of her juices and the darkest chocolate money could buy. She pressed herself into his face. Just as her orgasm was to explode around his tongue he began to withdraw, still licking slowly. Fair enough, she thought. She had little doubt that she would come soon. And that it would be good. He picked up the spatula again, this time handing it to her. She could take a hint. She led him to the only chair in the room. He tugged on his cock as she delved into the bain-marie, loading the spatula, and running back to him, her breasts, stomach and hips jiggling as she moved.

"Hands away," she instructed as she held the spatula

high above his cock, allowing the chocolate to drip slowly onto the erect tip. She saw it flinch slightly. No doubt it felt warm on his sensitive glans. Then it trickled down to his tight blond curls. Once his cock was suitably covered she knelt in front of him, and began to taste. He held her head, loosening her ponytail. Her hair fell around her cheeks. She developed a rhythm, sucking, licking, feeling him harden as she did so. She cupped his balls. They were tightening. He was close to coming. He pulled her head back up. Good. His instinct was the same as hers, she thought. She wanted to come with his cock filling her. And she suspected he wanted the same too.

But he wasn't ready yet, apparently. He pulled her up on to his lap, turned her so that she straddled him. His cock rubbed against her pussy. It felt like some kind of extremely pleasurable torment. So near, yet so far. She wriggled against him, quite sure that if she wriggled hard enough he would disappear inside her, the residual smears of chocolate easing his passage, and then she could ride him hard, not allowing him to stop until he'd come deep inside her. But she resisted. For now. She smiled at the thought of him bearing her weight, but he didn't seem to notice. He fumbled with her bra strap, finally flicking the clasp open and discarding her bra somewhere near his clothes. Then he buried his face in her breasts, holding the weight of her pale flesh in his hands, admiring how they were too much for his hands, spilling to either side of his palms. He tugged on her nipples with his teeth, causing her to gasp with that sweet mix of pleasure and pain that she loved so much. Then, suddenly, he stopped, looking towards the door.

"Hi, Craig."

Craig, Clara thought. Who the fuck is Craig? She turned to follow his gaze. Standing just inside the door was a second leather-clad figure. It dawned on her that he'd come to collect the éclairs. He was a carbon copy of the one whose lap she was sitting on right now. He stepped across the room.

"Hi, Joel, having fun?"

Clara shook her head. Did that extra-dark South American chocolate have hallucinatory qualities?

"You could say that. I've found myself the sweetest woman."

Joel ran his hands over the folds of her hips and stomach, giving each thigh a sharp slap. While Joel was distracted Clara attempted that wriggle she'd thought of a few moments ago, and it worked. She smiled at Joel as he slipped effortlessly inside her. He looked surprised, but not reluctant. She moved against him, and his hands, holding her hips, began to move her backwards and forwards, slowly at first, then with increasing speed. Her breasts bounced in front of him, and she giggled as he tried to catch them with his lips, like bobbing for extremely large and full apples. She reached for her pussy, parting her lips, ensuring her clit would rub against him, giving it the tiniest rub with her finger too, just to make sure. She glanced over her shoulder. Craig was closer now, and there was a telltale bulge in his tight leather trousers. He was beginning to unbutton them and delve inside with his right hand. Like most men, Clara thought, he couldn't resist a little touch.

"There's more than enough of me for two," she said. Craig knelt beside them, one hand playing with his now released cock, the other cupping her buttocks. He seemed able to keep up with their rhythm, his hands flying over his erection. Clara gasped when his left hand parted her arse cheeks. He circled her arse hole before pushing his forefinger slowly up inside her. Clara could barely control herself now, her orgasm close to peaking, her whole body quivering and shaking with desire. This was just too much. Better even than devouring the richest, sweetest mille-feuille and sweeping the tiny flakes of pastry from her lips with her tongue. This image excited her further, and she could no longer prevent her cunt spasming round Joel's cock, feeling the irresistible waves rolling through her, starting deep inside, only dying away once they'd left her body. In return Joel thrust still harder, no doubt unable to resist the pull of her cunt. And Craig twisted and turned his finger in her arse. This was like being in the best cake shop in the world. One in which the best cakes were being replenished as soon as they were devoured. Once their orgasms were complete, Craig pulled his finger from her arse and, holding her waist, he turned her round so that her back was to Joel's chest, her legs spread over his thighs.

"She's all yours, mate," Joel said.

"I most certainly am, Craig," Clara grinned. Craig lifted her from Joel's lap, hampered by his trousers and her weight, and staggered towards the counter. She wrapped her thighs around his waist. She was ready for him.

"Do you like buttercream?" she whispered in his right ear. He looked at her askance. He'd obviously never tried it.

"No worries," she replied. "We can experiment with your favourite embellishment." And then she gasped with pleasure as his cock worked its way into her welcoming cunt.

Once the boxes had been dispatched Clara dressed herself and began to wipe down the counter. She had no regrets. Tomorrow she would confirm her account with the courier company. But she wasn't too sure she'd bother getting that buzzer fixed.

Private Dancer
by Carole Archer

Allison was having a quiet evening in front of the TV when her husband James walked in and slumped in the seat beside her.

Putting her arm around his shoulders, Allison asked, 'Tough meeting, sweetheart?'

James nodded in response. 'And as usual they ended up in that bloody seedy lap dancing club in town. I told them I didn't want to go and they said I'm obviously under the thumb and not allowed to go. So of course I had to stay to show them they're wrong. Then all they do is throw themselves all over those scrawny women. I might as well not even be there. And I wouldn't care but those girls aren't even attractive. Most of them are like a bag of bones. And all those guys have wives, but they're totally forgotten about once we're in there. I refuse to cheat on you. I love you. And even if I wanted to cheat – which I never would – it certainly wouldn't be with some cheap, scrawny little tart in a dirty, seedy bar.'

Allison smiled and kissed him on the cheek. 'But it wouldn't be cheating. I'd understand if you wanted to watch the dancers for a while, I certainly wouldn't be offended. It must be nice to look at someone with a nice figure for a change.'

James looked genuinely shocked. Allison was

absolutely gorgeous, much more beautiful than those thin and unattractive women. He told her so, but she looked unconvinced.

She loved her husband dearly and knew he felt the same about her. And she was more than confident that he loved her voluptuous figure as much as anything else about her. But she couldn't blame him if he was attracted to those dancers with their perfect bodies.

She found it hard to understand that despite James having such a dominant personality, he backed down so easily to pressure from the guys at work and really let them get to him. She knew he hadn't been in the job for long and was trying hard to fit in, but she wished he would stand up to them for once.

She hugged him tight, kissed him passionately, then asked if he'd like to go to bed. His anger was soon forgotten once he got his hands on the beautiful body of the woman he loved. He caressed her curves and kissed every inch of her gorgeous body before making long, slow love to her.

Several weeks later James had another meeting. He'd warned Allison that he might be late, but said he would try to get out of going to the club. She thought that maybe he secretly enjoyed going and his protestations were just for her benefit, but she really didn't mind.

James truly didn't like the club but yet again found he was pressured into going with them. Once they arrived, all his colleagues went off to private rooms with the dancers, so he decided to go home and see if Allison was in the mood to cheer him up again.

He texted her to let her know he was on the way home, and said he'd call in the shop to get a bottle of wine. He was surprised when he received no reply from her, and there was still no reply when he phoned her. He was even more surprised to find the house in total darkness when he arrived home.

He opened the door, locked it behind him and started to fumble for the light switch. His wife's voice cut through the darkness, telling him to sit down, she'd be with him shortly, but to leave the lights off.

Puzzled, he slowly made his way to the settee and sat down. Allison called out to him and asked how his day had been. He complained that the management committee meeting yet again ended up in the lap dancing bar and, as usual, he was totally bored. He said he couldn't see the point of the meetings as they didn't discuss much work at all, and he believed it was just an excuse to go into town, and to the lap dancing bar in particular.

Allison turned on the music then walked into the room. She already had a bottle of wine chilling, and she brought him a glass. She said she would join him in a minute. He wondered if his luck was in, and he believed it must be when she started to massage his shoulders. He quickly began to relax and forgot all about the guys back at the lap dancing bar and their failed attempts to yet again make him join in.

His massage stopped all too soon, and Allison walked across the room and used the dimmer switch to turn the lights on low.

She walked around to the front of the settee, and he was stunned to see his wife in the tiniest red dress he'd ever seen, with her ample breasts spilling out. She was obviously wearing a push-up bra and her breasts looked bigger than ever. The bra was at least a cup size too small and the sight of her ample assets made his cock harden.

He longed to stand up and kiss her, fondle those huge breasts that he loved, but something told him to stay where he was.

He looked open-mouthed at the tight dress that clung to her curves, showing off her well-rounded stomach. He absolutely loved this and wished she would wear tighter clothes more often as he thought she looked so sexy. The dress clung to her hips and he longed to run his hands over them. The dress was also indecently short, and he clearly saw her black panties as she turned her back to him. She walked across the room and it was then that he noticed the pole.

His cock was already hard from the second he saw her in that dress, but as she started to do the sexiest pole dance he'd ever seen, just for him, no room full of perverts to share this one with, his cock got painfully hard. She turned her back to him and slid down the pole, her dress riding up even higher and her buttocks pushing out of the tight black panties.

He absolutely adored her bottom. In his opinion it was definitely her best asset. He loved larger women, he always had. But his favourite part of a woman was her bottom, and the bigger the better. He hated to hear Allison complain about the size of her bum. He believed there was nothing sexier than two full, round bottom cheeks bouncing seductively as a lady walked. And the way his wife's bottom wobbled around as she moved made him breathless with excitement.

He loved to spank her bottom playfully. He loved how the flesh rippled in response to his firm hand. He loved the softness of her bottom cheeks. It made him so horny lying beside her and fondling those buttocks, giving them the occasional gentle smack and watching them wobble. All these thoughts filled his head as he watched her bottom, and he longed to touch her.

Unable to stay still any longer, he put his glass of wine

down and walked over to her. She'd just slid up the pole again, but her dress remained scrunched up above her panties. He squeezed her bottom cheeks, which were bulging out of the very tight panties. She slapped his hand away and told him to sit down, no touching was allowed. Before backing away, he gave her right buttock a smack and smiled as the flesh wobbled in response.

He reluctantly moved back to the settee and sat down, shifting uncomfortably as his cock formed a noticeable bulge in his pants, literally begging to be released.

He wondered if he should give himself some relief and started to unfasten his zip. Hearing the zipper over the sound of the soft music, his wife turned to him and took his hand.

'I think someone would like a private dance in a private room.' Smiling and kissing him softly, she gently fondled the bulge at the front of his pants, which seemed to grow even bigger as he gasped with a mixture of both pleasure and pain.

She led him by the hand up the stairs, wiggling her bottom as she walked. He couldn't resist giving her another gentle smack, and he was almost tempted to push her down on the stairs and make love to her there and then.

When they reached the bedroom she kissed him passionately and started to remove his clothes. She knelt down in front of him, removing his boxer shorts, and his cock sprung free. She kissed it gently and ran her tongue along the length of it, then pushed him down onto the bed. His head was spinning and he desperately wanted to take her now, but she left the room and told him to wait.

A few minutes later the music started up again, this time coming from the stereo beside the bed. The room was in darkness but he could see the silhouette of his wife standing in the doorway. Using the dimmer switch she again turned the lights on halfway and started to dance in front of him. Now she was wearing a bright pink bra covered in sequins with long tassels hanging from the nipples. She was also wearing a sarong which matched the bra, with even longer tassels.

She started to do a belly dance and her breasts and tummy wobbled in time to the music. He was mesmerised by the sight of his beautiful wife and he moved forward to sit on the edge of the bed.

She moved her hips and the tassels on her sarong danced. Her breasts bounced and the tassels from her nipples spun round and round, almost hypnotically. He reached out to her and she took his hand, letting him pull her towards him. He put his hands on her bottom, enjoying the feel of her satin knickers and delighting in the feel of her large bottom cheeks. He squeezed them and ran his hands up her body. She still swayed in time to the music and her tassels brushed against him.

Allison's hands reached between her breasts and unhooked the front fastener on her bra, letting her enormous breasts spring free. Wanting to show her what her dancing was doing to him, James took her hand and placed it on his hard cock. She smiled and kissed him, bringing his hands up to her breasts and encouraging him to play with them.

He squeezed her nipples then covered her breasts with kisses, gently pinching her nipples between his teeth, rolling them in his mouth and sucking until she gasped with pleasure.

Kneeling down between his legs, she started to wank him slowly. He was desperate for relief and begged her to go faster. But she slowed down and started to kiss the end of his cock, taking it into her mouth and sucking gently.

When he was fit to burst, she stopped and moved away. She threw aside her bra and continued her dance, her breasts jiggling around as her hips swayed and the tassels on her sarong doing their own dance.

She cast aside the sarong and continued to dance in only her panties. James gazed at her huge breasts, the natural curve of her waist and the fullness of her hips and thighs. He watched her tummy wobble gently to the music and her breasts jiggle enticingly. He was more turned on than he'd ever been and he needed to take her now, but he didn't want to spoil what had obviously been very well planned.

She turned her back to him and bent forward. She grasped her ankles and spread her legs, letting him see that her new panties were crotchless. He gasped and reached his hand out towards her. She moved away, turned to face him and slowed her dance down, caressing her body as she moved, pushing her breasts together and gasping with pleasure as her nipples hardened and swelled.

She moved her hands away and her breasts continued to sway, despite the slower pace of the dance, and when she turned her back to him and wiggled her bottom, her buttocks bounced seductively. He reached out to her again and simply said, 'Please.'

His voice was filled with so much desperation that she relented. His wife was normally quite submissive and shy, so she shocked him by pushing him backwards onto the bed and straddling across him. She was so wet that his cock slipped easily inside, and she continued to tease him by sliding slowly up and down his shaft.

He grasped her hips and kneaded the soft flesh in his hands. He squeezed her buttocks and pulled her cheeks apart, pulling the flimsy material of her crotchless panties as much out of the way as he could. He reached around and slipped the end of his finger into her bottom, and she gasped loudly. She continued to ride him, trying desperately not to let his finger slip out. It was slightly awkward, though, and she again concentrated on giving him pleasure.

Leaning forward and letting her breasts brush across his face, she cried out with her own pleasure as he caught her nipple between his teeth and started to nibble gently, then sucked it not quite as gently. She tried desperately to seduce him for as long as possible but they were both frantic by now.

He rolled her on to her back, ripped off her panties and plunged his cock deep inside her. Within seconds his cock twitched and his body tensed as he had the best orgasm he could ever remember.

Rolling on to his back, he lay gasping for breath and sweating as he wondered if this was really happening to him or if he was about to wake up. His wife kissed him gently on the mouth and asked if he was OK.

He pulled her into his arms and kissed her, running his hands up and down her body, enjoying the feel of her soft skin and delighting in her curves. 'I love you, thank you so much.' Realising he'd been selfish and not satisfied her, he rolled her on to her back and went down on her, flicking at her clit with his tongue and plunging his fingers deep inside her.

She was close to orgasm when she begged him to hold her. With one arm around her shoulders he held her close, kissing her passionately, as his other hand stayed at her pussy, fingers thrusting in and out of her then stopping to rub her clit. It didn't take long for her to reach her own orgasm and, after she'd calmed down, she lay breathless in his arms, thanking him over and over again.

When they'd both got their breath back she asked if she was anywhere near as good as the dancers in the bar. Sitting up he looked at her, stunned. 'You're joking. They're truly awful. You're a million times better than they could ever be, and you're so sexy. I'd rather watch you any day.'

Smiling, he promised to put a good word in for her with the management of the club if she ever fancied a part-time job.

Laughing and shaking her head, she told him this performance was for his eyes only, and that next time he was sitting in the club longing to go home, all he had to do was think about his own private dancer, and he never knew what might be waiting when he got back.

Love at First Light
by Harriet Hamblin

Rum and raspberry, lavender and spice – the enticing aromas encouraged Cassie to pause in the doorway of the little shop. Handmade candles of every hue and shape lined wooden shelves against the walls.

Her gaze fixed on the glowing wicks of a cluster of lilac and cream. The pale flames flickered in the draught as Cassie took a step forward. She glanced across to the counter and the male assistant acknowledged her with a friendly greeting.

"May I help?"

"I'm just browsing," she said.

He reached to a shelf behind him. "I have what you're looking for." He placed on the counter a fat, round candle, the colour of beeswax.

Intrigued that he presumed to know her taste, she said, "But how do you know what I want?" She lifted the candle to inhale the exotic perfume and glimpsed his smile from the corner of her eye.

"Ginger: clears the mind for decision-making."

How did he know that she found shopping such a trial? Most women loved it. She held the ginger candle to her nose for a touch longer than necessary while she gave him a quick once-over.

He stepped from behind the counter, and she followed

his lean-hipped body over to the group of candles that had first caught her eye. His hand hovered for a second, and he sent her a thoughtful glance before picking up a square, cream one.

As she took it, his fingers brushed briefly against hers. "Imagine a tropical island."

She imagined his long fingers smoothing vanilla and coconut oil over her naked body. This made her smile. "Mmmm. Palm trees, sand and sun."

"Light this for an hour or two before bed and you'll sleep as if you're on holiday."

How could he know that sleep eluded her most nights? She'd tried everything and anything to relax. A scented candle wouldn't make any difference.

"I'll take it." The words were out. Too late to change her mind.

As she reached the door, he called out, "Come back next week. I'll have exactly what you need."

But needing another candle was as likely as taking time off work for a holiday in Fiji. *As if.*

Next week, she was back at the shop. The same man greeted her warmly. "You're looking very refreshed."

"I am sleeping better," Cassie admitted, as a flush of heat crimsoned her cheeks.

"That's good. It's great to see you again." His smile made her heart flip. "Hey, I'm sure you won't be able to resist this new candle I have in stock. Lemon and lime – guaranteed to stimulate your … er," his sage-green eyes held hers, "… love life."

Cheeky bastard. "There's nothing wrong with my love life!" But then, in a fit of conscience at her bare-faced lie, she bought the darn candle anyway.

A few days later, she called in to choose an

engagement gift for a friend. He asked some relevant questions about the betrothed couple which led to further questions, irrelevant, about herself. Now he knew her name and she'd learnt that his was Stefan. And that his former girlfriend had moved away up north.

Half an hour had gone by before it dawned on her that she'd virtually told him her whole life story. She'd been unable to resist his flattering attention. This had never happened to her before, but, she thought ruefully, he was simply so easy to talk to.

She'd led him to believe that she was 'between boyfriends' but the truth was that, actually, she'd sworn off guys for the foreseeable future. Her teasing work colleagues crudely described her as 'gun shy'. They were right. Men were just too much effort for too little return, in her unlucky experience.

Except for the most eligible ones, of course, and they seemed to be squeezed and snatched off the shelf as quickly as loaves of freshly baked bread.

"How about a box of these as a romantic gift for your friend?" suggested Stefan, as he floated several flaming, glossy, heart-shaped candles in a wide, shallow bowl of water.

Cassie, breathing in the heavenly, rich chocolate fragrance, glimpsed his face reflected in the small pool. She wondered why Stefan was still single. He was gorgeous, self-assured, caring and, as she caught his eye, practically psychic where she was concerned.

"That's so right for her. She'll love it!" Laughing, she turned to face him. "Are you this successful with all your customers?"

Inclining his head close to her ear, he whispered, "Only the sexy ones."

In that instant, as if she herself were made of candle

wax, her sensitive inner core melted into liquid heat. When he turned away to answer the phone, she took full advantage of the opportunity for a dignified exit.

For the next three weeks, Cassie went to the shop and, each time, purchased a candle that was exactly what she needed, even though she often didn't know she needed it until she was there.

She liked Stefan, liked his personality, enjoyed his company, but was in serious danger of becoming curiously addicted to his candles. She, who hated cluttering up her furniture with stuff, began to envisage candles eventually taking over every spare inch of available surface. Enough was enough, she decided. Her next visit to the shop would be her last.

Stefan was busy with customers when she arrived. After a short time, he excused himself and strode towards her.

"Cassie, today I have a very special one for you." His eyes sparkled as if he'd discovered a winning Lotto ticket down the back of the sofa.

Butterflies fluttered against her ribs as she allowed herself to be led through the door into the private staff room at the back. Her eyes widened as he offered her the tall, elegant candle, patterned in deep swirls of crimson and black, topped with a golden wick.

A deep scent of dusky red roses possessed her as she held it in her hands. Cassie closed her eyes and gave a sigh of pleasure.

"You like it?" Stefan enquired gently.

She opened her eyes to meet his intense gaze and the butterflies ran wild, like children on a windy day.

"I ..." Her throat went dry. "I have enough candles."

"Keep it," he urged, "as a gift. Now I'll tell you why it's special." He paused, making sure he had her full attention. "Don't light it until you're ready for love because the flame has the power to attract your most secret heart's desire."

The shop bell jangled. She blinked and he was gone.

Cassie, once home, put the candle in her spare bedroom, firmly out of temptation's way. She didn't really believe in all that mumbo jumbo, but, until she knew in her own mind what her true heart's desire was, she dared not leave it up to fate. This time, *she'd* be in charge.

The following night, a storm blew up. Rain thundered on the roof and wind gusts shook the house. Cassie ran to each room, snatching the windows shut. Just as she closed the curtains in the spare room, the lights went out and the house was plunged into darkness. She opened the curtains a chink to let in the street light, but all was a smothering pitch black.

A power cut.

Disoriented by her sudden blindness, Cassie stretched her arms out and felt her way around the wall. Her bare toe stubbed against the dressing table as her stumbling fingers closed around a smooth wax shape. A box of matches lay in a dish nearby. Scattering the thin sticks in her fumbling haste, she struck a light and put it to the wick.

A thin flame sizzled into life. *Uh oh.*

She waited for a week for something to happen, but, as she'd expected, no handsome stranger crossed her path, no lover swept her off her feet. She was surprised that she felt vaguely disappointed, somewhat disillusioned, and was even a little bit angry with herself for feeling anything at all.

She waited another week.

Same dull routine.

Unaccountably incensed, teased beyond endurance, she threw the candle back into her bag.

"You promised me passion!"

She thunked the candle down onto the shop counter. But as a slow smile spread across Stefan's face, Cassie felt suddenly mortified by her words. Her skin burned, prickles crawled along her neck. She hadn't known that she had wanted passion, let alone voiced it out loud. She'd thought she was happy enough, had everything she needed. Till now.

"You lit the candle," Stefan murmured, his eyes seeking hers.

Cassie's heart beat a painful tattoo against her ribs.

"I hoped you would." He reached for her hand. "You didn't know what you needed."

Perceiving that, for once, he wasn't referring to candles, she raised a sceptical eyebrow. "And you did?"

"Oh yes." His face grew serious. "From the moment I met you I wanted you. And I knew that, someday, you'd discover you wanted me, too."

Desire sizzled all the way down to her toes. Mesmerised by his beautiful eyes, she forgot to breathe. Fire fanned across her skin. She gasped and pressed her free hand to the cleavage of her pale pink soft angora jumper.

"Hey, don't hide those plumpalicious babes," he growled softly.

"Plump?" Her eyes narrowed. Did he mean fat?

He reached out to trail one finger along the back of her hand, sending a bolt of pleasure between her thighs. "Just like creamy ripe peaches."

Mmmm. Her favourite summer fruit. He wrapped his fingers around hers to lift her hand away. His lips parted and she caught a flash of teeth. A wild image of him sucking and nipping her tingling nipples leapt into her mind. Her heart thumped as he pressed his lips to her hand, his gaze burning with a come-hither smile.

Stepping out from behind the counter he flipped the sign on the door to 'Closed' and murmured, "Are you sure you're ready for passion, Cassie?"

Oh God. She closed her eyes. *Was she? He wants her, she wants him ... but now it was only a matter of time before he noticed her other ultra curvy bits ...* She sucked in her stomach. *Oh God!*

Her eyes opened as he drew her into his arms.

"Are you?" she countered, despite the rock-hard evidence pressing against her thigh. She moistened her dry lips with her tongue.

His head bent forward as if to kiss her. But instead his whisper against her ear took her breath away. "Hell, lovely, my wick's aching for the touch of your flame."

She gulped. *Oh God, he was ready, all right.*

But this man was different from any other she'd ever met. So she shouldn't have been so shocked when Stefan grasped her by the shoulders and stepped back, stooping to peer into her face. "You find it hard to trust men, don't you."

He made it a statement, not a question. *Oh God, he must have felt her knees shaking.* She stared at him. How did he understand her so well?

"I'm not surprised after what you told me of that last boyfriend of yours." He shook his head as if disgusted. "My old man was a lot like him; charming one minute and in a foul temper the next." He shot her a lopsided grin. "Fortunately, I only inherited the charming bit."

Cassie grinned. "Makes you a good salesman."

He shrugged. "Sometimes." His hands slipped down

her arms in a firm caress. "But work is the last thing on my mind right now."

A throb of pleasure quivered deep in her vagina at the naked intention in his gaze. She squeezed her thighs against the sweet ache but it was useless to resist. He was her true desire and they both knew it. She grasped his hand and led him to the back room.

"You're so lovable," Stefan breathed as they both sank down to the floor. Cassie giggled and playfully pushed him on to his back on the cherry red carpet.

His eyebrows shot up. "So you want to be in control, do you?"

She poked her tongue at him and he groaned, burrowing his hands under her top. He pulled her full length on top of him, capturing her in a kiss that took her breath away. She threaded her hands through his silky black curls as he covered her cheeks, her brow, her nose and her neck with feverish kisses. She drew his lips back to hers, opening her mouth for him, their slick tongues entwining in an exquisitely torturous man-woman dance.

"Touch me," he groaned, his hands shaking with need as he dragged her top over her head. She undid her bra and flung it on to a desk, laughing as he lifted his head to bury his face in her breasts. "You smell good. Touch me," he said again, reaching for his pants zipper.

"Uh, uh," Cassie teased, covering his hand with hers. "Don't be in such a hurry."

She squeaked in surprise as he flipped her on to her back and straddled her, pinning her with his strong thighs. A shiver ran through his voice as he drawled, "Lovely, just for you, I'll take you nice and slow."

He lifted himself off her, his hands pushing up her skirt and stroking her thighs. The heat of his touch built and built till the thudding of her pulse screamed: *Now! Take me now!* She half sat and reached for his zipper, easing it over his straining, thick cock.

Tearing off his shoes and socks, his trousers and underwear quickly discarded, he knelt at her side, his hips jutting forward. His eyes fluttered closed as she bent her head to press her lips against his erection's velvety smooth skin. She flicked her tongue up the thick shaft, circling the tip, licking up a bead of glistening sperm.

"Fuck, you're good," he rasped. She glanced up to see him watching her, his eyes glazed in ecstasy. She bowed her head again but he stopped her. "Make me wait, lovely. Make me beg for it." Cupping his hands on either side of her face he captured her lips in a slow-burning kiss.

Desperate to ease the sweet throb building between her legs, she slid her fingers under her knicker elastic to explore the slippery softness of her vulva. She moaned against his mouth, her fingers slick with juice.

Without breaking the kiss, Stefan slipped his own finger along the edges of her elastic. She squirmed against him and with one quick movement he wrenched her knickers down and poked one long finger right where she craved.

"You're so wet, my lovely," he murmured against her lips. She gasped as he pulled off her skirt and laid her back against the floor. Hastily she covered her exposed love handles with her hands.

"Relax," he growled, lowering his mouth to her nipples and sucking each one in turn.

Her clit screamed for attention but all he did was push her legs up, spread them wide and sit back on his haunches.

A cold draught of air fanned across her hot moistness as he gazed at her vulva. "Beautiful."

Cassie groaned, reaching for him. "Lick me, suck me,

stick me, just *do* something, dammit."

"I thought you wanted to …"

"I know what I want," she interrupted. "And I need you *now*!"

Stefan laughed and bent his head between her legs, his tongue hotly searing her clit, lapping at her juices, feathering the delicate skin at the top of her thighs.

She arched her back, writhing as wave upon wave of pleasurable, white-hot agony washed over her, leaving her quivering.

He shucked off his shirt. Dreamily, she raised a hand, trailing it languidly across his chest, swirling the dark hair in one finger and pinching one tiny, brown nipple.

He groaned and caught her hand, straddling her, holding her gaze as he parted her folds with his other hand and pushed in his cock with one thrust of his hips. Her eyes widened. He was *very* big.

"Fuck, you're tight," he whispered. "Beautiful and small – I'm going to stretch you, my lovely."

Small. This made Cassie giggle; it seemed strange that he was so lean on the outside yet large where it mattered, while she was quite the opposite.

She put her arms around him and buried her face in the fresh smell of his neck. It was ten times more fragrant than any candle.

He rocked against her, his breathing rapid, and she braced herself for his orgasm. But he withdrew and offered his penis for her to suck.

As she drew his full shaft, slick with her own juice, into her warm mouth, she raised her eyes to watch the pleasure transforming his face. "I'll put him back inside you soon," he promised. "Stop when I say …" He tensed, his face contorting with the effort of control as he gasped, "Now!"

She withdrew and cradled his stiff cock in her hand, guiding it down to between her thighs. "Nice and slow now, big boy."

He eased in and then held his body still. Desire trembled in his gaze as he rasped, "Sorry lovely ... I can't ... wait ..." His eyelids lowered, and his breath quickened as he thrust his hips forward. And water sprang to her eyes – damn but his gun was *BIG*.

Cassie wrapped her legs around his back, his spasms jerking her spine into the soft carpet. She hugged his weight to her as his breathing slowed, huffing a sigh of protest as he withdrew. She wanted to stay connected for ever.

Stefan tugged his shirt off the office chair and laid it across her. She sent him a sleepy smile of thanks and snuggled under to absorb his manly scent.

He pulled on his trousers. "Hey, lovely, thank you for coming ... in my shop."

She smiled at the double meaning. "I was like a moth drawn to the flame."

"I knew you couldn't resist a stiff candle."

They both laughed. Then she said, glancing around for her knickers, "But there *is* something you *don't* know."

"What's that?" Stefan dropped a kiss on her forehead.

Her pulse danced. "That investing in candles is the best decision I've ever made!"

He said nothing. Her certainty plunged to the pit of her stomach. She bit her lip. Had she said too much, too soon?

Stefan seemed to be lost in thought. She held her breath. Then his face cleared and his eyes shone. "You, Cassie, are the light of my life."

Heart in meltdown, she jumped into his arms.

Princess Beatrice
by Sadie Wolf

Stephen
I loved watching Beatrice when she was naked. It was rare to find a woman who was so comfortable in her own skin, so content to expose herself to my gaze.

Lying on her side on the bed, her body lit by the morning sun and her long auburn hair in ringlets, she looked just like a painting. Her forget-me-not blue eyes and her rosebud mouth made her look innocent and pretty, but her pale peaches-and-cream complexion bore the telltale flush of recent sex.

Her sidelong silhouette dipped in at the top of the waist and curved out to wide, sexy hips. Her thighs were big and smooth and soft, an ocean of unblemished white skin contrasting deliciously with the burnt umber of the triangle of neatly clipped pubic hair.

Not for the first time I wondered, if I had met Beatrice first, before marrying Helen, would I have been happier? But I pushed the thought out of my mind: I am married, I have children and my family comes first.

Sadly, it was as if mine and Helen's paths had diverged over the years without either of us noticing, and now we had virtually nothing in common. Once she was warm and kind but now she was sharp and spiky. She used to be soft physically too, but since joining the gym with a friend she had become increasingly obsessed, spending every spare moment there. Helen's body had become hard, a rail-thin ironing board covered only with rock-hard, lean muscle. The cuddle had gone out of her.

Hence I found myself in Beatrice's bed. Beatrice's bed was warm and welcoming, Beatrice's body was soft and sensual, and after a year of exploring every delicious inch of her voluptuous body I was crazier about her than ever.

Not that I would admit all this to her. She'd probably run a mile. She wasn't the kind of woman who sat by the phone waiting for my call. She went on dates, saw other men. She was a free spirit. It's what I loved about her ... actually, I found it quite sexy ...

'Daydreaming, are you?' Beatrice looked at me from under her lashes.

'Only about you.'

Mark

I always specify 'more to love' in the Looking For section. So many women nowadays are either too thin or are always on a diet, and that turns me off. I like the ones who advertise themselves as plus sized; I usually find they are happier with themselves. And so they should be: so many men are like me and have a liking for a larger lady. I like breasts and I like softness, I don't hold with all this gym and work-outs business for women.

I met Beatrice in the usual way – on the Net – and although I thought she looked sexy in her photograph, she looked a million times better when I saw her in the flesh.

She walked, or rather *sashayed*, into the bar, hips swinging, red hair flying, and I swear every man in the place stopped what he was doing to stare. She was wearing one of those skirts that cling on the hips and bum and flare out to the knee, with nice shiny high-heeled boots, and she had on a low-cut sweater that her tits were just bursting to escape from. Honest to God, I was rock hard even then.

She invited me back to hers and into her bed that very first night. I must've done something right because I've been back on a regular basis ever since. Even taken her away on trips. I know I'm not the only one, she's got some married lover, and who knows, maybe there are others too, but I'll settle for what I can get.

Beatrice
I can honestly say that I've got my life exactly how I want it. I lived with someone for seven years, but it didn't suit me. I forgot what music I liked, what my favourite foods were, even who my friends were. One day he just walked in and opened his mouth and told me it was over. I almost passed out with shock and the thoughts in my head were all, how will I manage, how will I cope on my own after all this time? But even then, underneath the terror, was a hard, shining glimmer of hope, of utter relief that at last I had been set free.

Stephen
Seeing her smile made me want to make love to her again. It was almost eleven and I really should have been going, but I never could resist that smile. I kissed the tip of her freckly nose and ran my fingertips along the curve of her side-lying body, feeling her skin shiver with pleasure. That too drove me wild: the ease with which she came alive under my touch. I rolled her over on to her back and she looked at me with her lovely blue eyes and bit her lower lip. The way she anticipated the pleasures of the flesh so prettily was something I found irresistible.

I began to stroke around the outer edges of her

tremendous breasts and she sighed, settling herself into her pillows like a cat. Her delicate pink nipples began to harden, and I let my fingers work their way inwards and begin to gently stroke the fullness of her breasts until I came at last to her hard little nipples and began to tease and tweak them in just the way she liked. She sighed again and looked up at me from under her half-closed lashes. The colour had begun to rise in her face again, giving her a pretty little blush on her cheeks. She could never hide her arousal, she was far too sensual a creature for that.

I let one hand wander down from her breast, over her ribcage and on to the soft swell of her belly. I rested it there, feeling the soft warmth of her body under the flat of my hand, as my other hand still worked on her breast and nipple. I felt the anticipation in her body, the tension of her waiting for my next move. I kept her like that, suspended, for as long as I could bear and then I very slowly slid my hand down from her belly and down between her legs, opening her soft fleshy thighs as I did so. She moaned softly, opening her legs for me as the tips of my fingers made contact with the delicious wetness there.

She was putty in my hands, as always. It drove me wild, this sense that she was utterly in my power, that she would probably do anything in return for my providing her with sexual relief. When she was soaking wet, and all my fingers were glistening and slippery, I decided it was time to fuck her.

I sank into her like a starving man falling on a banquet, even though I had made love to her less than an hour before. Her body had that effect on me, the softness of her thighs and belly, the almost obscene abundance of her creamy breasts and the sheer burning heat of the inside of her body. I wanted to drown in her body, to suffocate myself in her flesh. She was a siren, a temptress against whom I was powerless.

Then I opened my eyes and saw her pretty, delicate-looking face, her blushing cheeks, and I saw that she too was helpless in the face of her sexual desire. I slowed down and focused on taking her slowly and steadily to orgasm. I felt like the most powerful man on earth.

Mark

I arrived at her place with flowers, as always. She opened the door to me, wearing a plain, dark blue dress that clung to her curves and was low enough to give me a glimpse of cleavage and short enough to give me a view of her legs to just above the knee. I sat down on the sofa, and she brought me a glass of wine. Her place was full of photos and pictures, with rugs on the floor and cushions everywhere, a real woman's place. She sat down beside me, her pale, freckled arm inches away from me, her red hair done in beautiful ringlets that made her look old-fashioned and sexy at the same time. I felt like a very lucky man. I wanted to do something to show her that.

'Will you let me take you away on your birthday? We could go to a show in London, maybe stay for the weekend?'

She smiled and put her hand lightly on my arm.

'That's so kind of you. But I really don't know what I'm doing yet.'

Shit, what an idiot! Of course, I wasn't the only man in her life, was I? I got the distinct impression from the little I had picked up that the married guy was very well off. He was probably taking her to a five-star hotel in Paris. I couldn't compete with that.

'I really don't know what I'm doing yet,' she said

again. 'I'll let you know, OK? Thank you.'

She stroked my cheek, leaned over and kissed me on the mouth. Her lips were soft like petals and her mouth tasted clean and sweet. My irritation evaporated. Of course a woman like her was going to be in demand, and she had never led me to believe that we were 'exclusive' as they say nowadays. I put my hand on her huge, glorious breasts and wondered what this other man was like. Did he touch her the same way I did? Did he appreciate her properly? What was his favourite part of her body? What did they *do* in bed? What did it *look* like?

She stood up and took off her dress. She looked fantastic, all boobs and huge, sexy hips, all wrapped up in raunchy red lacy underwear. Of course I had to share her, I could hardly expect to keep such a creature all to myself.

She unbuttoned my trousers and sank down on her knees on the rug, and I felt like I would shoot my load right there and then just at the thought of what was to come. I shut my eyes and got a hold of myself. When I opened my eyes, I saw her huge breasts spilling out of their bra onto my lap and her red ringlets, pale, sweet face and sexy red mouth going down on my cock.

Beatrice loved to suck cock, you could tell. Some women just love it, it's not a chore or a favour for them, it's more like they're simply born to do it. As if there's nothing in the world they'd rather do than get a cock in their mouth and suck it. Her lips were soft and her tongue was very warm and wet and the inside of her mouth was smooth and velvety. She moaned and pressed her breasts against me as she got into it. She liked it when I held her head, pulled her hair and pushed my cock into her.

She must suck his cock too. Lucky guy, married guys don't get too many blow jobs as a rule. The thought of her sucking his cock turned me on quite a bit for some reason, and my mind drifted on to them fucking, him taking her from behind, her sitting on him, this faceless, nameless man whom I knew next to nothing about. But it was arousing, picturing her doing it with him, and I spurted into her mouth much quicker than I intended to.

Beatrice
OK, so I knew I was taking a bit of a risk, introducing my two lovers to each other. But it's my birthday. Mark had been increasingly curious, and Stephen had been increasingly clingy, and I didn't want him to get any silly ideas in his head about leaving his wife. And for both of them, I thought it was time to take our relationship to the next level, sex wise. I mean, what is the point of having two men if you can't have a threesome once in a while?

I arranged for Stephen to arrive first. I was more worried about how he would handle my proposal than Mark. As usual he was nicely dressed in an expensive shirt and his almost-grey hair was newly cut in a neat, short back-and-sides style that suited him. He was carrying an enormous bouquet of lilies and a present. He looked so pleased to see me that for a moment I wished I'd made tonight just about the two of us. He stepped indoors and I saw him do a double take as he realised what I was wearing – a white faux-fur coat and new, expensive Agent Provocateur black underwear, including stockings and suspenders and a pair of blood-red skyscraper heels. I'm quite a restrained dresser usually, but I thought that tonight I needed all the help I could get.

'Anyone would think it was *my* birthday. Happy birthday, beautiful.' He kissed me and handed me the present, a square box wrapped in silver paper. Inside was a beautiful silver and sapphire necklace.

'It's perfect, thank you.'

'I brought champagne.'

'Perfect.'

'So, what are we doing tonight?' Stephen sat down and drew me on to his lap. His eyes were sparkling and I could feel him hard under my thighs. I wrapped my arms around him and kissed him full on the mouth, passionately enough, I hoped, to take his breath away.

'Well, you know how it's my birthday and I can do whatever I like? Tonight we are going to play ... at sharing.'

'Sharing?'

Right on cue, the doorbell rang. I got up to answer it without a word, letting my coat fall off as I did so and leaving Stephen's mind to work out what was going on.

Mark's eyes looked like they were going to pop out of his head when he saw me. He too was carrying flowers and a present. I felt like a very lucky girl, and the evening hadn't even started yet. He had hardly stepped through the door when I wrapped my arms around his neck, pressing my ample bosom against him and kissing his neck. I took hold of his hands and looked him in the eye.

'Stephen's here.'

'What, but –'

'It's OK. I invited him.' I gave Mark my naughtiest look and after what seemed like for ever, his face broke into a smile. I knew it, I just knew he'd be up for it.

'You dirty little minx. Go on then, I guess you'd better introduce us.'

I wondered if that's what swingers parties were like, everyone standing around making small talk, pretending they were there for some entirely innocent reason. Mark managed to strike up a conversation with Stephen about the congestion charge while I poured everyone champagne. The whole thing was somewhat surreal, me in my sexiest underwear and the two of them looking and not looking and sizing each other up while being mercilessly polite. I wanted to fast forward to everyone being drunk.

However, to my surprise, Stephen came to the rescue. He cleared his throat, as if he were about to make a speech.

'Well, Mark, I'm guessing this isn't exactly what you had in mind … it's as much of a surprise to me too, although I knew that Beatrice, well, I knew I wasn't the only man in her life. But the fact is it's her birthday, so I'd just like to say that I'm not going to raise any objections to whatever Beatrice has in mind … I suggest we all just relax and go with the flow, so to speak.'

'Fine by me, mate. How about a toast. To the birthday girl.'

'To Beatrice!'

We clinked glasses and, as if by magic, the awkwardness had gone. Mark stepped forward and kissed me, and we were snogging, and then he broke away and sort of *handed* me to Stephen, who kissed me, and I could feel him trembling. I took his hand and led him over to the sofa.

Once we were sitting down, I could feel him relax. His hands found my breasts and slipped inside the fabric of my bra and touched my nipples. He kissed me long and hard. I felt down with my hand – he was hard for me. I looked up. Mark was sitting watching us and looking fairly relaxed. I smiled at him.

'Stephen, I think you should put Beatrice over your knee, for being such a naughty girl and being so greedy,' Mark said levelly.

Stephen smiled. 'Really? What do you think about that idea, Beatrice?'

I wriggled on to his lap, face down. My heart was beating hard against his thigh. 'I think Mark's right. I have been a very naughty girl.'

Stephen bent forward and whispered in my ear. 'Are you sure? I don't want to hurt you.'

I turned my face towards him and kissed him on the mouth. 'You won't. Just do it.'

I turned back and looked at Mark, who held my gaze steadily. I held his look, calming myself. Inside I was full of butterflies.

Stephen pressed one hand firmly between my shoulder blades before bringing the other down hard on my bottom. I shouted out in spite of myself, and he brought his hand down again, harder this time, jolting me so that I bit my lip. I opened my eyes. Mark was looking at me with blazing eyes. Stephen brought his hand down again and again, on my bottom, on my thighs, harder each time, literally knocking the breath out of me as the force of his blows threw me forward against his legs.

I realised that Stephen was probably showing off in front of Mark; perhaps he thought I got spanked by Mark on a regular basis and that this was therefore some kind of competition. But the truth was I had never been spanked like this and it was a revelation. As I began to ease into the rhythm and the sensations of it, I began to be aware of the burning heat between my legs, the wetness of desire that was making the insides of my thighs all sticky.

At last, Stephen stopped, apparently exhausted.

'Are you OK?' he whispered solicitously in my ear.

'Mmmm.'

'Feel how wet you made her,' I heard Mark say.

I held my breath: I didn't know if Stephen would take kindly to the way Mark seemed to be playing it, telling him what to do. But Stephen just laughed and said, 'Is that right, that made you wet? You are a funny girl, my hand feels like it's about to drop off. Still, each to their own ...' He trailed his fingers down my thighs and lightly grazed the outer edges of my pussy. I gasped. Stephen laughed again. 'Well, Mark, you're right. I have to tell you, I had no idea she liked that kind of thing ...' He slipped his fingers effortlessly inside me and I moaned out loud, incapable of controlling myself. 'I must say, I'm really not sure what to do with you ...'

'Fuck her up the arse.' Mark's voice had a distinct edge of excitement to it.

'Really? Do you think she'd like that?'

'I *know* she would.'

It was true, I had had anal sex with Mark.

'Do I need some ...'

'Lube. There's some in the bathroom, I'll get it for you.'

I lay down flat on my belly on the carpet while Stephen put on a condom and lube. Mark lay out on the sofa, a broad grin across his face. He watched as Stephen slowly and gently pushed his cock inside me. It was very tight and the first part was always the worst, but once he was in I relaxed. I heard Stephen's breathing becoming shallow and excited and more than once he bent forward and bit my shoulder hard as he kissed me. It was good to feel him so excited, good too to feel Mark's eyes upon us, glassy and shiny with desire, crisscrossing my body, concentrating hard on every little detail of the proceedings.

'I have to say I'm getting more than a little hot over here, do you mind if I make use of her mouth while you're occupied back there?'

'Be my guest,' said Stephen.

And then Mark was getting up and unbuckling his

trousers. He lay down on his side in front of me, his big hard cock just in front of my mouth. I smiled at him and opened my mouth. I had everything I could have wished for.

Where Phone Sex Can Lead
by Deva Shore

'Brad, hi,' I said, pleased to hear his voice again.

'Hey, Carmen, how are you?' he said.

'Great. What sort of story would you like to hear today?'

'None. I just thought you might like to chat again.'

'That's sweet but these calls are expensive.'

'No problem. I have the money and the time.'

'How about you give me your number and I'll call you at home?'

And that's how it all began. I'd started my own business about six months ago. Guys would ring in, I'd ask them what type of sex story they wished to hear, they'd chose and I'd read it to them. Some companies had recorded audio tapes but I preferred to read them live and my customers like it that way too. Business was booming. I was surprised and pleased at its success.

Brad was actually my very first customer. Over the six months he was also the most regular. In between readings we'd chat. Cost him a fortune but he never complained, so I finally decided to take it one step further. He seemed like a nice guy.

I must admit as I dialled his home number I felt just a bit excited. I hadn't had a boyfriend now for nearly two years and whenever Brad called I'd feel those stirrings, that little tingle you get when you're keen on someone of the opposite sex.

Over the next few weeks we got to know each other quite well. I found out he was a successful lawyer and that he hadn't had a girlfriend for quite some time as he was always busy at work. I think he'd been burnt and wasn't eager to get into another relationship too quickly.

There were some days where we'd chat for hours. He was so easy to talk to. I told one of my girlfriends and she said I was crazy. Not good for business. While I was talking to him I allowed other clients the opportunity to meet other operators. I was losing money she said, and for what? She said he was probably getting his rocks off now for nothing, free of charge.

I was offended and hurt by her comments.

'Nothing will ever come of it,' she said. 'You're wasting your time.'

'But he sounds so sweet and sincere,' I said.

'He's probably old, bald and a pervert. Stop calling him.'

In the end I stopped calling *her*.

Brad and I advanced to a new level fairly quickly. He asked me intimate questions and I didn't even hesitate to answer. Neither did he. Pretty soon there wasn't much we didn't know about one another.

When he asked me what I looked like, I hesitated. I didn't want to turn him off so I lied. Said I was five feet nine inches tall, blonde with perky breasts and a slim figure. Said I looked fabulous in a micro-mini and sometimes did a bit of modelling on the side.

I knew he was impressed.

He sounded absolutely gorgeous. Said he was dark with short hair, blue eyes, a dimple in each cheek and just over six feet tall. He worked out at the gym four nights a week and was a conservative dresser.

He was a lawyer with a big firm in the city. Said that was why he could afford all the phone charges. He had a great personality and I found myself totally relaxed and open with him but when he suggested that we meet I panicked.

'No! I don't think that's a good idea,' I blurted out.

'Why not? I'm dying to see you face to face,' he said.

I gulped. I wanted to meet him too but I'd lied so dramatically about my looks that I just wasn't game. I was five foot nine and blond but that was all that was true. Instead of perky breasts I had huge melons which were so big that if I wasn't wearing a bra they'd hang down to my waist. I'd never worn a mini skirt in my life ... they didn't make them that big and I wouldn't have worn them even if they did. I was large all over.

I was happy though. I didn't care about my size and was comfortable with myself but I always got those stares and comments from other women, as though being me was unacceptable. Over the years I got used to them, heard them all, but now that Brad wanted to meet me, well, I didn't want to disappoint him.

'Look,' I said, 'I haven't been quite honest with you.'

'What? You're not married are you?'

'No.'

Boyfriend?'

'No.'

'Lover?'

'No,' I said sighing.

'Well, what then?'

'I'm not as good-looking as I led you to believe,' I said quietly.

'I don't care about your looks. We get on famously. I'm not one of those shallow types. Believe me I won't judge you by your appearance.'

'I don't know.'

'Look Carmen. You're being ridiculous. After all this time I thought you'd be able to trust me enough to believe that?'

'I do, but I just don't want to disappoint you.' I said softly.

'You won't. Trust me, I'm a lawyer, remember. Er, strike that last sentence,' he laughed.

'You're sure?'

'Just give me your address and I'll take you out tomorrow night and give you a night you'll never forget.'

So I did. I gave him my address and for the first time my phone number too. He said he'd call me with the details tomorrow. When I hung up I noticed my hands were shaking. I really liked Brad. I liked him a lot. I decided to ring another friend, Mary, and confide in her.

'Are you nuts?' she screamed down the phone line. 'You're not going are you?'

'Yes,' I said. 'I am.'

'Did you tell him about your weight problem?'

'I don't have a problem with my weight. It's the rest of you that do,' I said, slamming the receiver down on the cradle.

I was fuming. Who the fuck did she think she was.

The next morning Brad called.

'I've got a limo booked and I'll pick you up for dinner at the Ritz at seven thirty.'

My God, I thought. The Ritz. He must be loaded.

'Really?' I said. 'I'm impressed.'

'And so you should be,' he laughed.

'I'll see you then,' I said, hoping I was doing the right thing.

'I can hardly wait,' he replied.

I was nervous. I took more care with my personal

appearance than I've ever done. Pampering myself with a pedicure, manicure and facial. After showering I moisturized my whole body, dabbed myself with perfume and dusted my skin with a lightly scented talc.

I chose red underwear, a silky black pants suit with a sexy see-through camisole.

As I was dressing I had a critical look at myself. I thought I had a fantastic body and wouldn't change it for the world. I loved my tits with their darkened areolas that surrounded and drew attention to my gorgeous nipples. I loved to caress my own breasts, loved the weight of them, they way they swayed when I walked, loved the way guys would bury themselves in them. It always turned me on, made me feel very sexy.

I had great hips and a nice rounded stomach. I always thought I would have loved to have been a model for a sculptor or a painter, someone artistic who would appreciate my beauty. My thighs were curvaceous and when I put my hand there the heat emitting from them was amazing.

I had a little Mohawk of pubic hair and the rest of me was hair free, waxed to perfection. All guys loved that.

I turned to look in the mirror.

'Great arse,' I giggled.

Guys loved to grab handfuls of my flesh, love to squeeze and jiggle it. They also love to bury their faces between my thighs. Just thinking about it had me wet with desire.

Glancing over at the clock I saw that I had one hour to go. I inched on my underwear, slipped into my outfit and pulled up my hair, pilling it high on my head but leaving soft wispy stands to frame my face. I used only a small amount of make-up and a thick smear of red lipstick, the exact shade of my underwear, on my pouting lips. As I lay down my brush the doorbell pealed throughout my home.

Butterflies fluttered in my stomach. Taking a deep breath I wrenched open the front door. Brad was everything he said he'd be. Tall, dark and handsome, oh so handsome. He had a big bouquet of red roses cradled in his arms and even though he had a smile on his mouth it didn't reach to his eyes.

He was disappointed. I knew it.

'Hi,' I said shyly.

'Great to finally meet you,' he said, thrusting the flowers into my arms.

He followed me in while I put them in a vase. I wanted to hide the tears that were smarting my eyes and threatening to spill down my cheeks.

Composing myself I turned to him, 'Ready?'

He took my hand and I gasped when I saw he really had arrived in a limo. He helped me in and we sat in silence while he opened a chilled bottle of champagne. We both drank quickly and by the time we arrived at the restaurant we were feeling more relaxed, well I knew I was, that was for sure.

Sitting down in the chair that Brad had pulled out for me, I saw some of the other diners staring at us. Brad did too. I noticed the look of confusion on his face.

'Don't worry,' I said. 'I'm used to it.'

'To what?'

'People staring at me because of my weight,' I whispered.

'You're kidding. I thought they were looking at me, at how handsome I am,' he joked.

'Yes, well that too,' I laughed.

'Let's drink to a great friendship and a wonderful dinner,' he said, raising his glass.

I sipped slowly wishing he'd toasted to a night of wild and unadulterated sex.

The evening went brilliantly. The fact that the other diners kept staring seemed to be to my advantage. Brad became very flirtatious. As though making an effort to silence their stares. Me, I loved it. We ended up having a fantastic night. We got on famously and on the way home I asked him in for coffee.

'That would be great,' he said.

Filling the kettle up with water, Brad moved in behind me. He kissed the back of my neck. I was so surprised I nearly dropped the kettle.

'You don't have to do that,' I said, feeling as though he was only going through the motions.

'I know,' he said, taking the kettle to place it on the sink so he could grab me and turn me around into his arms.

He lifted my chin, lowering his head to kiss me. I looked deeply into his eyes, saw them crinkle mischievously and then he was all over me. His tongue deep into my mouth and his hands roaming all over my body.

I pushed my pelvis into him, pleased to feel he had half an erection and even more pleased when I heard a low murmuring deep in his throat. His hands grabbed at my arse, then up my back, before one slipped up my camisole and over my breast.

'Oh God,' he whispered, his mouth on my neck and working its way down. 'Where's the bedroom?'

I dragged him back with me, stumbling as we began to tear each other's clothes off. We fell onto the bed, both shirts gone and he landed between my open thighs staring down at me. He pulled the camisole off and his eyes devoured my breasts. He lunged for them, like most men do, burying his face into the cleavage. His hands slipped beneath me, his fingers unhooking my bra. He peeled it down my arms and threw it on to the floor.

'They're magnificent,' he said, smiling. 'Absolutely magnificent.'

He crushed each of them, pushing them together, nibbling at my erect nipples before sucking one gently into his mouth. I held his head with both hands, barely able to believe this was happening.

He stood, dropped his trousers and his jocks together. He kicked off his shoes, staggering as he pulled off his socks. I giggled when he flung off his trousers and stood naked before me. He had the most enormous cock I've ever seen. Not only was it long but it was thick. Real thick. The knob was bobbing up and down, precome already oozing from the slit.

He smiled at me when I finally managed to tear my eyes away from it and then he was tugging my pants and panties down together over my shoes. I lay there naked before him wearing only my stilettos, quivering in anticipation.

'You're beautiful,' he said, 'just beautiful.'

I blushed, pleased and feeling as horny as hell. It had been a long time.

'Open your legs,' he commanded.

I did.

'I can see your pussy lips glistening with your juices,' he whispered, as he lowered his head towards me.

'My shoes,' I muttered.

'Leave them,' he insisted. 'They heighten my desire.'

'Oh,' I whimpered, unable to hide my own lustful feelings.

Lying between my open thighs he opened up my outer lips. 'You smell beautiful too,' he said, diving down to lick at them.

Within moments he was munching madly, licking long and hard, then nibbling delicately on my clit. I lifted my feet, placing my shoes on the bed so my knees were bent high before I dropped my legs wider open. He nuzzled in further, his fingers exploring me and I came quickly but quietly not wanting to do anything to break the spell of this amazing encounter.

He looked up over my mound, grabbing my arse, my hips, his fingers digging into my flesh. I ground my pussy up into his face, loving it but wanting more. I wanted his cock deep inside me and I didn't think I could wait another moment.

Pulling his head up towards me he climbed up my body, his wet mouth leaving tracks where he'd been until he reached my mouth. I dragged him to me, tasting myself on his lips, licking his cheeks, his face before I thrust my tongue deep in his mouth as he thrust his magnificent cock deep into my pussy.

I was so wet he slid in, full to the hilt, my clit rubbing up against his pubic hair as he ground into me. He lunged for my breasts squeezing them while fucking me ferociously. I began screaming, unable to control myself as he fucked me harder and harder.

Wrapping my thighs around his back I kicked the heel of my stilettos into his arse cheeks. This spurred him on further until I was coming like never before, my breasts arching towards him where he attacked a nipple, sucking it hard into his mouth and as I came he bit down on it, pulling it away from me so I grabbed his head and held him close as my sweet juices gushed out of me and over my bed.

He laughed, 'You fucking horny bitch. Here, roll over on top of me.'

In one swift movement I was impaled upon his mighty cock. I placed my hands on the wall and lifted myself, looking down between our bodies as his cock; glistening wet as it eased its way out. Then I slammed myself back down, over and over, riding him harder than I've ever ridden a cock before.

I just couldn't get enough. I came over and over, with him pulling, crushing and devouring my tits. Nothing was enough. My juices spilled out of me, all over him and still he fucked me until I thought I'd pass out. With my legs quivering I disengaged myself and flew down to his cock.

Barely able to circle his shaft with my fist, I lowered my head to lick at his shiny knob. The veins were straining under the tightness of his skin. I ran my tongue over them feeling them pulse beneath it. I looked up at him, desire and lust all over his face. Opening my mouth wide I sucked him in, my fingers playing with his hairy balls before slipping further to tantalize his puckered hole.

'Oh man, that's fantastic,' he said.

'Hmm,' I mumbled, my mouth full of cock.

His hand stroked my hair, 'That's great. You'll never know how great but I want your pussy up here. I wanted to lick you while you're sucking me.'

Manoeuvring myself around, I lowered my pussy over him while still sucking his cock. He grabbed my hips, dragged me down, smothering himself into my hairless flaps. I sucked harder as his tongue found my clit and within minutes we were both coming, neither able to stop.

I rolled from him, collapsing beside him. He turned around and gathered me into his arms. Smiling at him, I ran my finger down the side of his face.

'I suppose you'll be leaving now,' I said.

'Not on your life,' he said. 'I'm never leaving. I've never desired anyone so much in my life.'

'But I thought …' I trailed off.

He silenced me by kissing me, both of us tasting ourselves on the other's mouth.

'Now that I've found you I'm never letting you out of my sight,' he said, holding me tightly.

We've expanded our business now. I do phone sex too. I take calls but now when I'm talking dirty he's in bed with me, and when I'm telling some guy on the phone what I'd love to do to him, I'm actually doing it to Brad. And he does the same for me. We have great sex, better than you could possibly imagine and we're getting paid while we do it.

What a life and thank God for phones.

Wanted, Exhibitionists
by Jennie Treverton

The main reason why Greta replied to the ad on the noticeboard was to shock her two colleagues at the college library. Despite the fact that they were both reed-thin, or rather, because of that fact, Bethan and Yvonne were both weight-obsessed, constantly comparing exercise regimes and the nutritional value of their lunches. Greta wouldn't have minded that in itself, but what she did object to was their attitude towards her, a modestly overweight woman. She objected to the way they'd hush up whenever she came within earshot, as if they'd been talking about something that she mustn't hear. She objected to the meaningful sidelong glances they'd exchange. They seemed unable to relate to her, a woman with forty-four-inch hips and a forty-inch, E-cup bust who had butter and cheese on her jacket potato. Sometimes she found herself itching to take a pile of the books she was shelving, slam them down on the inquiries desk and shout at the two of them, 'I'm not a monster, you know, I won't eat you!' Not a scrawny pair of chicken wings like them, anyway.

One day, just before the end of autumn semester, the college library was particularly quiet and Bethan and Yvonne's discussion of their competitive starvation was drifting along the bookshelves and provoking in Greta, tidying up the Plastic Arts section, a continuous low level of irritation until, suddenly, she had an idea.

She stood up straight and sauntered down the main aisle, swinging her long red hair and generous hips. She stopped at the noticeboard opposite the inquiries desk. Bethan and Yvonne watched her silently.

'Have you seen this ad?' said Greta, pointing at the noticeboard. 'A student put it up last week. I've been mulling it over and you know what? I think I'm going to give it a go. Sounds like it might be fun.'

She read the wording out loud: 'Wanted, exhibitionists for exciting and potentially controversial art project. Must be comfortable in own skin. Contact Stevie Smith.'

She reached over the desk, took a pen and a Post-it note, copied down the number on the ad, then picked up the desk phone and dialled.

'Hi, is that Stevie? I saw the poster in the library and I'm interested. Yes, well I hope so, I'd like to think I am anyway. No, evenings are best. Tomorrow, six pm. I know where you mean. Do I need to bring anything? OK. No problem. Oh, the name's Greta by the way, Greta Featherton. Okay, bye now, bye.'

She put the phone down and smiled in an off-hand way at her colleagues before going back to her tidying. She felt very good indeed, and when Bethan and Yvonne began to mutter it was so quiet that Greta barely registered it.

The next day, after work Greta went to the art block. Outside the entrance a petite girl of about twenty in battered jeans with stripy rainbow tights showing through the rips was lounging against the wall and smoking a roll-up. The girl's head was shaved apart from two short curls, one in front of each ear, plastered to her face with hair cream to form stylised sideburns. She had black eyes and a serious expression. Greta recognised her from the library, she was in there often, straining under the weight of piles of outsize art books.

'Hi, I'm Stevie,' she said without smiling. 'Thanks for coming.'

They walked briskly through a succession of empty classrooms with paint spattered on the floor and tables, the whitewashed walls hung with students' artworks, the corners cluttered with half-finished sculptures, bent wire animals, featureless polystyrene heads.

'I like your look,' said Stevie as they walked. 'You're like a Rubens but your hair makes you more like a pre-Raphaelite or even a Klimt. Nice.'

'Will I do, then?'

'Absolutely. Look, I need to ask you a couple of questions so I know how to approach you as a subject. They're personal but don't take them personally. Firstly I need to know if you're gay or straight.'

'Oh, most definitely straight,' said Greta.

'Right, that's fine. And I need to know how you feel about nudity. You should know up front that I need you to be nude for this.'

'I thought you would. It's not a problem,' said Greta, who hadn't done anything like this before and, although nervous, was quite looking forward to showing herself off.

'Good,' said Stevie. 'Because I'm about as serious about this project as it's possible to be. I'm going to be a famous artist. Thousands, maybe millions, of people are going to see your body. You need to be comfortable with this.'

As far as Greta was aware, nobody from Vale College had ever made it big in anything. And art was the most dead-end subject of them all. So she was more than a little sceptical about Stevie's words, but didn't let on. She had to admire the girl's ambition.

'Here we are,' said Stevie as they banged through another set of double doors. 'I've booked this studio. We won't be disturbed.'

Unlike the other rooms there were no students' artworks here. The windowpanes were whitewashed along with the walls so nobody could see in or out. Around the edge of the room was an array of technical equipment and two video cameras on tripods. In the middle of the floor was a brown leather reclining armchair, and facing it was a large television on a stand showing a pornographic movie.

'Why don't you get undressed,' said Stevie.

While Greta took her clothes off Stevie sat cross-legged on the floor, taking each garment as Greta handed them to her, until Greta stood before her naked and feeling a little giddy. Stevie gestured for Greta to sit in the armchair, which she did, the leather cold and squeaky against the spreading flesh of her bottom.

'You're not going to paint me then,' said Greta, looking around.

'This isn't a painting. It's an installation.'

'A what?'

'An installation. It means I'm going to film you.'

'Oh right,' said Greta who was becoming slightly mesmerised by the porn over Stevie's shoulder. Two men, one black, one white, were doubly penetrating a tanned blonde with spherical tits and an expression that suggested equal parts ecstasy and anguish.

'So, erm, what are you going to call this installation?' said Greta, attempting to stay focused.

'*Onan Twelve*,' said Stevie.

'Oh right,' said Greta.

The trio were lying on their sides, the blonde holding a

leg in the air so the camera could pan in close to her bright red cunt and supple perineum. The two cocks were shunting in turns. Ignoring the porn, Stevie carried on talking in her serious, intellectual way, explaining the aim of her art using language Greta couldn't hope to understand. The black man's cock withdrew from the blonde's anus and sprayed blobs of semen all over her back. Greta tuned in to Stevie to hear her say, '... and from you I'm hoping an honest response to these materials, these erotic materials if I can term them that way.'

'Oh,' said Greta. 'Does that mean what I think it means?'

Stevie nodded. 'Yes,' she said. 'I want to film you while you masturbate.'

'Oh right,' said Greta.

'Are you comfortable with that?' said Stevie.

Watching the black man's three fingers poking where his cock had been, Greta said, 'I think so, yes.'

'Great,' said Stevie, jumping to her feet. 'Let's get started.'

She arranged Greta's legs so they were wide apart, one draped over the arm of the chair, and then went behind the chair to recline it fully.

'Just relax,' she said, switching on a bright light.

Greta watched the white cock shoot spunk all over the blonde's inner thighs. She was acutely aware that her exposed cunt was responding wholeheartedly to this odd situation, tightening its inner grip and becoming rather wet. She looked down at herself and her starkly lit naked body seemed unfamiliar, as if it was someone else's body, someone else's mounds and valleys, as plump and smooth as satin cushions. Her coppery red hair lay in trails over her shoulders and around her breasts.

'Nearly ready,' said Stevie from behind a camera. 'You can start fondling yourself if you like. Now, I'm not recording sound, so you can talk to me if you need to, but please don't turn round. I'll give you directions as and when. Oh, and one thing. If you feel like you might come, you must let me know before you do. That's crucial, okay?'

'Right,' said Greta.

'I'm going to start the bubble machine now,' said Stevie.

'The what?'

Stevie switched on a black box which began spewing iridescent bubbles all around Greta.

'I just thought it would look cool,' said Stevie. 'You have amazing breasts, Greta. Can you touch them a bit?'

Greta began to caress her tits, lifting their heaviness in each hand, perky nipples peeping through her fingers. The porn switched to a different movie. A good-looking naked man with wavy dark brown hair was sitting in an armchair just like the one Greta was on and wanking while watching something off-screen. He was slim and Greta could see all the muscles and tendons of his shoulders working hard under his slightly freckled skin. Before she knew it Greta's hand had travelled down to her pussy and pressed apart her plump folds. Her clit was fat and greedy and she began to rub it with two fingers.

'Good,' said Stevie.

Greta supposed that the man was another participant in the project. She thought he was gorgeous. Dark-haired and dishy, just her type. A vein bulged on his fine forehead. She was amazed at how tight his ball bag was. He must have been right on the edge of coming. His cock head was angrily scarlet, his fist a flurry on his shaft.

'Your thighs are closing,' said Stevie. 'Keep them

open if you can.'

Bubbles were falling all round her, bursting on her skin and leaving soapy patches. She ran her free hand over her curves and was delighted by the slipperiness. Imagining that the man was watching her at the same time as she watched him, she began to finger-fuck her vagina, digits pumping with loud squelchy sounds.

'Who is that man?' she gasped.

'He's Onan Eleven,' said Stevie.

The man's face was pink and shiny with sweat. He stopped his stroke and gripped his cock just under the head, his other hand grabbing the arm of the chair, and he seemed to roar through clenched teeth. Greta realised he was trying to stop himself from spunking up. At this, her whole cunt began to spasm.

'God,' she said. 'I'm going to come.'

'Not yet,' said Stevie.

Greta took her hand off her pussy.

'No, keep fingering yourself,' said Stevie. 'This is continuous footage. You mustn't stop.'

Greta tried to touch her clit as delicately as possible but it was so difficult. The man on the television was in a similar state, clutching his cock as if it was in danger of detaching from his body and flying across the room.

'I can't hold off,' she whimpered.

'You must,' said Stevie. 'Just a bit longer.'

Greta put two fingers up herself, trying to avoid her clit as much as possible. It was hell and heaven, being so wet and soapy, so full of trapped arousal. She screwed her eyes up so she could hardly see the sexy man on the screen, and frigged her cunt with agonising slowness.

After what seemed like an age, she opened her eyes fully and saw that Stevie was now standing in front of her.

'We're done,' she said. 'Do you want to finish yourself

off or would you prefer a tongue?'

She said it in such a matter-of-fact way Greta wasn't sure if she was serious. But then she noticed that Stevie's fly was undone, her hand down the front of her own trousers.

'I'd love a tongue,' said Greta.

Stevie knelt before her, buried her stubbly head between Greta's soft thighs and sucked her cunt as if it was a dripping peach. Over her head Greta saw that the man on the screen was no longer alone but had Stevie's mouth clamped over his dick. Greta came immediately, with much groaning and thrusting and agitating of airborne bubbles.

After she'd put her clothes back on Greta asked Stevie, 'Can you just tell me again, what's the meaning of this thing?'

Stevie sighed and said, 'It's my reaction to the negative dialectic between the contemporary phenomenon of societal individuation and the immutable inalienability of the human experience, albeit situated within an idiom of inegalitarian discourse between Ur-man and Ur-woman.'

'Oh right,' said Greta.

Seven months later Greta arrived at work to find an envelope waiting for her. Inside was a gilt-edged card inviting Onan Twelve to a private viewing of an exhibition by Stevie Smith, the centrepiece of which was to be her 'critically acclaimed installation', *Onan 252*. Rather impressively, the exhibition was to be held not at the college but at a real art gallery called Ephebe, thirty miles away in a posh part of the city. The invitation said to dress smart casual and be prepared to speak to members of the press.

She wore her hair long down her back, lots of bangles

up her arms and a black velvet dress that flowed over her hips and only just hid her areolae. Ephebe looked tiny from outside but was very long inside, with room after room stretching back, all of them packed with people sipping Prosecco and inventing things to say about the works of Stevie Smith on the walls. Greta tried not to think about the intimate knowledge of her own sexual response that was soon to be bestowed on these roomfuls. She sank a few Proseccos and felt a little better.

Wandering deeper into the gallery Greta noticed that Stevie's paintings and photographs seemed to show a preoccupation with condoms on pavements. Here and there she'd lock eyes with someone who looked as far out of their comfort zone as she was. As she entered the gallery's final room she saw, on a plinth shrouded in white linen, a large flat-screen television on standby.

'Hi,' said someone to her left.

The voice belonged to a tall, good-looking, freckled man. Onan Eleven himself, in jeans and a scruffy lumberjack shirt.

Until that moment it hadn't occurred to Greta that he'd be there. With his clothes on he looked a little older and hopelessly out of place. His curly hair had a charming semi-flattened appearance, as though he'd tried to tame it with a brush and given up. He had the slightly gawky air of an academic or a reclusive writer. She smiled at him, feeling herself blush from toe to scalp.

He shook her hand and said, 'You work in the college library, don't you? I've just started a photography course.'

'Really? I haven't seen you in there.'

'I only signed up last week. I popped my head in to check out the facilities and I saw you behind the counter.' He smiled warmly at her. 'Stevie recommended the course. She's a mate of mine from way back.'

'Wow, you're starting at the college. That's terrific news,' said Greta.

'It is, isn't it?' he said, looking into the dark cleft of her bosom. 'So are you involved with this Onan thing?'

'Well, erm,' said Greta.

She was saved from finishing her sentence by a surge of people entering the room, at the front of which was the artist, dressed in a black rubber catsuit slit open up her back to reveal bare skin painted swirly blue. Stevie wore the creamy expression of a woman who knew she'd brought a great many of the people around her to orgasm. A few press photographers stepped forward to take pictures and she posed with a typically unsmiling, rather confrontational stance. She fielded a few questions from scribbling reporters. A middle-aged man with a ponytail came to stand next to the television and called for quiet.

'Hang on to your seats,' he said, even though everyone was standing. 'I'm simply beside myself to introduce you all, without further ado, to the evocative, provocative *tour de force* that is *Onan 252*.'

He produced a remote control and clicked it at the television. The screen was filled with a confusion of reds and pinks, which revealed itself to be, as the camera slowly panned out, the gleaming entrance to a vagina. As if emerging from within it, the view widened until the whole cunt was shown. There was a vibrating movement around the top of the labia, the result of a fingertip engaged in vigorous stimulation of the engorged clit.

Greta didn't remember frigging herself as briskly as that and sure enough the cunt wasn't hers but belonged to Stevie herself, sprawled naked on the brown reclining chair and writhing with eyes tightly shut. Greta was surprised by the bushiness of her mousy-brown thatch. The camera panned out further and Stevie grew a frame around her, the frame of another television set. It took Greta a moment to work out what she was looking at, until the view had widened enough to show the television set and the brown recliner in the white studio. A punky-looking man was in the chair, tossing himself off while watching Stevie on the television. The view continued to widen until the punk was on the television and a stout older man was in the chair, wanking while watching the punk. Again and again the camera drew back to show different women and men masturbating on the recliner, each of them aroused by footage of the previous link in the masturbatory chain.

There was Onan Eleven, every bit as sexily tense as Greta remembered, his cock just as unruly. And then she saw her own body, surrounded by wobbly bubbles as she sank her digits into herself, and she was relieved to find she was quite pleased with how she looked. Yes, she was plump, but there was something glorious in the way her curves bobbed and flowed. Her shoulders were softly rounded, her upper arms jiggling as she made love to herself, large breasts moving as if floating on water. Her thighs were pale and fleshy, toes curling with pleasure, pubes nicely trimmed, vulva shining. In the corner of her eye she saw Onan Eleven look from the screen to her and back again. Now there was a compact young Oriental man in the chair, leaning forward as he frigged his cock to the image of Greta on the television.

Nobody else was accompanied by bubbles but there were other interesting little touches here and there: a slender brunette was surrounded by piles of handbags that toppled over as she began to peak; a swarthy man with curly black hair and a gold hoop earring had a Weimeraner puppy lying at his feet; a well-groomed older woman was wearing a showgirl's headpiece made of peacock feathers. Stevie had filmed people of all colours, shapes and sizes, all in the advanced stages of arousal. There were fat bodies, skinny bodies, muscled bodies, wasted bodies, tanned flesh, dark flesh, porcelain flesh. Fake boobs, tiny tits, pendulous titties, an endless variety of nipples. Big cocks and skinny cocks with heads that were purple and scarlet and almost black, sometimes shining, sometimes spilling pre-come. Modest little clits and big fat clits that stuck out rudely like tongues.

After a while the incessant backward motion of the camera, the constant shrinking of image after erotic image, began to make Greta feel weirdly hypnotised. Because there was no soundtrack the gallery was deathly quiet, and she could hear heavy breathing all around. She looked away from the screen and saw uncomfortable expressions on everybody's faces. Hands were straying across trouser fronts, knees were squeezing together. Lust lay heavily over the whole room. Greta glanced at Stevie. Surrounded by her awestruck entourage the artist's eyes were fixed on the screen with mad intensity. Greta's eyes strayed towards Onan Eleven and she saw that delicious pink flush again, and an unmistakeable bulge in his jeans.

The film came to an end with Stevie in the chair again, climaxing with a long shudder of limbs. She stood up and walked towards the camera until the image became nothing but blurred skin. The picture went black. The gallery erupted with applause.

Greta's eyes met Onan Eleven's. He raised his eyebrows tentatively.

'Toilets,' she said and the two of them scooted through the crowd.

They found the gents' near the front of the gallery. Nobody was in there and they locked themselves into a cubicle, rushing to get under each other's clothes. While

Greta unclinked his belt and freed his thick cock he dived under her dress and peeled down her knickers, leaving a trail of moisture down her thighs. He sat on the toilet seat and pulled her on to him. Her wet cunt sucked up every inch of his dick and they began to fuck with brisk determination, his pubes tickling her clit, his hands pulling down the front of her dress, his mouth sucking on her nipples and biting her copious tit-flesh.

'Beautiful tits,' he said, voice muffled. 'Beautiful, curvaceous tits, arse, neck.' He looked up at her face, sank his hand into her hair. 'You're a work of art, Onan Twelve.'

She could hardly believe this man was inside her and she looked at him with incredulity, but it was him all right, she recognised the vein on his forehead, the way he gritted his teeth, the way his body shook ferociously as he threw himself into the moment of lust. The abandonment he'd displayed on the screen was in his fingers, digging into her flesh, and in the thrust of his cock and the smell of his body heat. Greta's knees hammered against the cubicle walls and their groans echoed up through the air vents and along the water pipes.

'I'm going to come,' he growled.

'Me too,' Greta moaned, and she bounced on him crazily, chasing the feeling as hard as she could until she was right on top of it. She had no desire to hold herself on the edge and plunged straight into her climax with a shriek. Immediately after she'd come he pulled out of her and shot cum all over her silky dimpled thighs.

As they quietened down they heard shouting and looked worriedly at each other. A clamour of voices in the gallery, someone barking orders, someone else protesting. Quickly they straightened themselves and left the cubicle.

Greta poked her head round the door and saw that

everyone was being herded out of the gallery by police. She tried to hear what people were saying and the odd phrase came to her: *censorship*; *obscenity*; *poor old Stevie*. With his hand on her arse they joined the flow and soon they were on the pavement with everyone else, the arty types and the Onans and the reporters and photographers. A television news crew had turned up.

Handcuffed and struggling, the pony-tailed gallery owner emerged into the street, dragged by two police officers.

'Brutality!' he shouted to the crowd as he was thrown into the back of the van.

Then came Stevie, also flanked by two officers but not in handcuffs. Evidently she had decided to co-operate with the police. Her face was shining with excitement, grinning from ear to ear. She saluted the crowd with a defiant fist in the air, and as she passed the television crew she beamed into the camera.

'She's a smart girl, is our Stevie,' said Onan Eleven as the police bundled the artist into the van.

In the Bakery
by Kristina Wright

Bernadette loved the mornings. As she walked the six blocks to Giovanni's Bakery and Café in Old Town, she adjusted her blouse and straightened her skirt, her pace quickening in time to her pulse. She had been working at the bakery for six months now. Vincent Giovanni was her boss, and the baker.

He was also her lover, of sorts.

Vincent was an iron-fisted taskmaster of a boss – a whirling dervish who demanded nothing less than perfection. Bernadette thrilled to the sound of his voice barking orders. In fact, she was the only one of the bakery girls who worked with Vincent in the mornings because she was the only one who could meet his demanding nature. The other girls – Tammy and Darla, Pauline and Esther – called Vincent a beast. Bernadette did, too. What the others didn't know was that Bernadette *liked* what a beast Vincent could be. It made her hot.

This particular morning, Bernadette was three minutes late getting to work. That required some doing on her part as she often left her apartment a full hour before she was due at work. Today, she dawdled around the corner from the bakery, looking a bit like a streetwalker, if whores wore white blouses and black skirts with sensible shoes.

When she finally slipped inside the unlocked back

door of the bakery, a variety of scents assaulted her. Baking bread and pastries filled the air with a heavy, sweet aroma; the heat was nearly oppressive. Her mouth watered. She had gained a few pounds since she started working in the bakery. Her boyfriend Simon had noticed – and enthusiastically improved. He told her she looked like a Rubenesque goddess and smelled like sugared heaven. She giggled at his florid descriptions, but she loved it just the same.

She paused to admire Vincent as he pulled trays of baked bread from one of three massive ovens. He wore white pants and a white shirt with the sleeves rolled up over his thick, muscular forearms. A white apron was streaked with red and purple – strawberry and blueberry from the morning pastries – and a dust of white flour adorned his thick, black hair.

"You're late," Vincent said, without looking at her. "A little morning screw for the poor boyfriend?"

Bernadette shook her head, realising that Vincent still hadn't looked at her, and found her voice. "No. Not today."

"Why not?" Vincent asked slyly. "Didn't he want you?"

Heat flushed her already warm cheeks. "Of course."

Vincent knew the intimate details of her relationship with Simon. She had told him. So he knew that Simon often awoke while she was getting ready for work and tried to initiate sex. Vincent didn't like the idea of her having sex with Simon before she came to work for him. It shouldn't matter whether he liked it or not since he was only her boss. And yet ... it did matter.

Bernadette hadn't indulged Simon's advances that morning because she was in a rush to get to work. But at night, smelling like sweet dough and cinnamon, she would roll around in tangled sheets and tell Simon how mean Vincent was to her today. The thought made her shiver.

"Good girl," Vincent said. "But you're still late. Third time in two weeks."

"Yes, sir," she responded meekly, suddenly thinking perhaps she should have been on time today. "I'm sorry, Vincent."

Vincent finally turned to look at her. His jaw was an unyielding hard line, and his dark eyes stared through her. "What happened the last time you were late?"

Her cheeks flushed hotly as she recalled, "I received five smacks with the oven peel."

"Bare-bottomed smacks," Vincent reminded her. "You squealed every time I struck that round little rump of yours."

"Yes, sir."

"Then I made you rub that wet little slit of yours until you came while I watched your ass redden. Remember?"

"Oh yes, I remember," she breathed. What she didn't tell him was that she remembered it every time she touched herself in the shower or in bed after Simon fell asleep.

"Whatever am I going to do with you, Bernadette?" The question was half exasperation, half fondness.

Bernadette lowered her eyes demurely to study the flour-dusted floor. "Whatever you like, Vincent."

"Precisely."

Vincent crossed the expanse between them. Before she had time to react, he grasped the front of her blouse and tore it, the buttons pinging off the steel stove fronts, one, two, three. She gasped, but kept her hands at her sides even as Vincent stared at her exposed bosom. Her white lacy bra barely covered her nipples, and she felt them harden under his scrutinising gaze.

"Oh yes, I think I know what needs to be done," he murmured, more to himself than her.

He hooked his thumbs in the cups of her bra and pulled the fabric down until her plump breasts popped from the confines of the lace. She glanced down, seeing her breasts sitting atop the underwire of her bra, the lacy cups bunched beneath them. Her nipples were dark and puckered. Aroused. She bit her lip to keep from whimpering and closed her eyes.

"Are your nipples sensitive?"

She nodded, though he already knew the answer to the question. He had asked it before – and tested her. "Yes, sir."

"Lovely."

She opened her eyes and watched as he walked to the enormous butcher-block table where various utensils lay. They were innocuous on their own – spoons and spatulas of wood and metal – but in Vincent's hands they could cause pain. He looked them over and then shook his head.

"These won't do." He walked back to her. "Go get two order clips."

She blinked at him.

"Now!"

She scurried away at his barking demand, going to the front of the bakery where the order clips were stored. Her breasts were still exposed and, though the bakery was shrouded in darkness, her first inclination was to cover herself as she faced the broad expanse of glass windows facing the street. But it was still dark and no one was out. At least not yet. She quickly grabbed two clips from the bin by the register and went back to Vincent.

"Good girl," he said, as he took the clips from her.

The bakery girls used order clips to hold the special

orders to the wall for Vincent and the assistant bakers to see. Four neat rows of white orders for bread and cakes and pastries hung clipped to metal cords lining the far wall. The clips were sturdy metal fasteners meant to last for years through repeated use. This time, Vincent did not use them for bakery orders. He used them on Bernadette's distended nipples.

The clips were cool against her fevered skin, but that pleasant feeling was quickly replaced by the bite of the clips closing around her nipples. She looked down to see the metal protruding from her breasts. The sight was embarrassing, humiliating and terribly exciting despite the slight twinge of pain.

Vincent admired his work with a smirk. "Do they hurt?"

She hesitated. If she told him the truth – that they hurt but were certainly bearable – he would find some way to make them hurt more. If she lied and told him the pain was excruciating, he would certainly realise she was lying and make them hurt more. Since she was already being punished for one indiscretion, she chose truth.

"Not worse than a pinch," she said.

Vincent grabbed the clips and tugged them until her nipples were stretched from her breasts. She winced, but held her stance as he continued to tug, testing the limits of the clips. Almost simultaneously, they popped from her nipples with a sharp snap as their metal pieces met again.

"How about that?"

She resisted the urge to rub her sore nipples. "That hurt, sir."

"Good."

Once again, he clamped her breasts. "You are a bad girl, Bernadette."

She nodded. "Yes, sir."

"I don't like to punish you like this but I'm starting to suspect you rather enjoy it," he said, as he tugged at the clips. "Do you?"

"Oh yes, sir!" She hadn't meant to confess her masochistic pleasure, but Vincent was driving her stark raving mad with the tugging.

The clips popped free from her nipples and she whimpered.

"Poor girl, your nips are sore now, aren't they?"

Again, she nodded. Hot tears pricked her eyelids and her bottom lip quivered. Yet her pussy – her naughty, betraying pussy – was wet.

"Perhaps you should kiss them and make them better."

She stared at him. "Vincent?"

"Lift them to your mouth and give them a kiss."

"I – I can't," she whispered.

Vincent went to the large buckets that lined the wall. Each contained a different fruit filling. He dipped a large ladle into the one labelled "Strawberry" and brought it back to her. With two fingers, he smeared strawberry filling on each of her tender nipples.

"You can't run around with strawberry jam on your strawberry nipples, girl," he said. "Better clean it off before it stains your blouse and I have to send you home to change."

The scent of berries assaulted her senses. The cool filling soothed her sore breasts. She licked her lips. Strawberry was her favourite flavour. She cupped her left breast in her hands and raised the ample mound to her lips. She licked at the strawberry filling on her nipple, lashes lowered so she didn't have to watch Vincent watching her. The jam was thick and sweet and she lapped at it like a hungry kitten after the cream.

"Good girl," Vincent praised. "Now the other one."

Bernadette didn't hesitate this time. She licked and sucked the strawberry flavour from her right nipple, her tongue almost as soothing on her abused flesh as the cool filling. Her breasts were clean now, but still sticky and sweet smelling. She looked at Vincent, eager for his next order.

"Have you learned your lesson about being late?"

Her lips twitched. She longed to say 'No' just to see what his response might be, but the time was slipping by and the bakery would be opening soon. She nodded.

"I'm not so sure you have," he said thoughtfully. "Take off your panties and sit on the table. Legs spread. Do it quickly. I can't spend all day disciplining my wayward staff."

She wasn't sure what she expected, but she obeyed. She slipped off her panties and laid them on the edge of the solid wood table. Then she hopped up on the high table, skirt hiked up so she could spread her legs. She fought the urge to close her legs and kept her hands balled at her sides as Vincent stared at her.

"You look like a most delicious tart," Vincent said. "I am quite certain you are a tart, aren't you?"

She nodded. "Yes, sir."

Vincent came toward her with another dollop of strawberry jam on his fingers. "Are you a strawberry tart, Bernadette?"

She shook her head.

He smeared the berry filling on her bare pussy. "Now you are a strawberry tart."

She wriggled on the table, feeling the jam slide down between her swollen, wet lips. Aching to relieve the building pressure in her cunt, she pressed her thighs together quickly and tightened her muscles. It wasn't enough, but for a moment it felt delicious.

"Stop that. Spread your legs and sit still."

She took a breath and did as he demanded. She was still holding her breath when he braced his hands on her thighs and spread them wider. The breath came out in a rush and a moan when he lowered his head and licked a line up between the lips of her pussy.

"Strawberry tart," he said, moving up to kiss her. "Taste yourself."

She parted her lips for his tongue, tasting the sweetness of the strawberry and the musky taste of her arousal. She whimpered into his open mouth, thighs quivering beneath his powerful hands.

Pulling away, he bent again to lick at her pussy. "You are dripping strawberries, Bernadette."

She waited for another kiss and was rewarded by the hard press of his mouth on hers. He brought his hands up to her breasts and rubbed his callused thumbs over her sensitive nipples. Holding them between his thumbs and index fingers, he bent again to her pussy. One, two, three more laps as he tugged and pulled at her nipples. She squirmed on the edge of the table, whimpering as the ovens rumbled and hissed behind her.

"More of you than the strawberries now," he said, rising to kiss her again. "You taste sweet, Bernadette. You taste like the bakery."

She whimpered at his slow teasing and kissed him wildly, sucking his bottom lip into her mouth, licking away her taste so that he would want another. She clutched at the edge of the table as he sucked each of her nipples into his mouth on his return trip to her pussy. Her thighs quivered in an effort to stay still as Vincent lapped enthusiastically at her wetness. She watched his dark head, still dusted with flour, working between her thighs. If this were punishment, she would have to find a way to be very, very bad every day.

Two things happened at once. The buzzer on the main oven sounded, announcing that a hundred or so loaves of bread were done just as Vincent sucked her slippery, swollen clit into his mouth. She arched her back and screamed over the sound of the unrelenting buzz, every muscle in her body straining toward a powerful, nearly painful, orgasm. As Vincent nursed her clit gently and tweaked her nipples with his rough fingers, she came. Spiralling waves of heat and wetness seemed to go on and on for endless minutes while the buzzer echoed her cries for more. Her orgasm rippled through her as Vincent continued to lap her sensitive pussy. Finally, he stood and gave her one quick, wet kiss before turning his attention to the business of the day. "Naughty Bernadette. If my bread is burned you are going to be severely punished."

As he went to silence the buzzer, Bernadette tucked her breasts into her bra and pulled her panties back on. Straightening her clothes the best she could, she slipped an apron over her ravaged blouse. She wondered what Vincent might taste like covered in strawberry jam. Or her wetness.

She nodded decisively. Next time, she would be ten minutes late to work.

Watching
by Victoria Blisse

The door is ajar, not by a great deal, if someone walked past not expecting the door to be open they probably wouldn't notice it but I am very aware of the fact it isn't closed.

There is a draft and I can feel it as a cold caress up my naked leg and it makes me wonder if someone may be outside the room. My stomach somersaults over itself but I do not move, I promised Todd I would do this. I take a breath and force myself to relax. I slide down over the strange duvet, the black satin covering my generous curves rising slowly up over my knee, exposing my rounded thighs and gathering at the small of my back. It uncovers my arse and sends an erotic jolt from my mind to my cunt.

I glance at the clock again and I realise I must not hesitate any longer and really I do not want to. I have waited for this for months, the long-distance words and pictures only stoking the flames of desire. The orgasms as he watched from his computer only satisfying me for brief moments. I've needed him here with me, watching me, hearing his breathing as he watches me; really watches me.

I use the fantasies of old to excite me. The text on the screen and the images he sent. His come on my photograph, his words caressing me, his passion for my body as he describes how he feels, how he wanks as he watches me. I remember his voice; rough with arousal calling my name as I screamed out, a plastic phallus inside me, my finger pressing with the exact pressure I needed to tip me over into the tempest of orgasm.

I hear his voice in my mind as I slide my hands over my voluptuous breasts. I can feel the hard, unyielding peaks beneath the soft give of the fabric and I squeeze my fingers together over each nipple, making them swell and pulse in time with the throbbing of my eager pussy.

I have never been able to tease myself. As much as I know he enjoys the slow build-up, I rip down the lacy frill and ease out my heavy breasts. Taking the flesh in my warm hands as I free them to the air, feeling once more the draft from the door, teasing the very tip of each nipple with its chilly caress. I warm them with my fevered fingers, trying to hold myself back, wondering if he is at the door already or if he's even in the hotel yet. Yearning for him to enter the room and be here with me.

Cool black satin crinkles and smoothes over the swell of my tummy as I shift my hand lower. Skimming over my stomach I ignore its soft contour as now I've teased myself enough. I gently stroke my hot inner thigh and part it, imagining my hand is Todd's and he's begging me to show him my erotic secrets. I would make him beg, the idea arouses me but he wouldn't have to beg for long. I want him to see me. I want to feel his breath on my wet parted lips as I slip my finger between them.

I imagine him there, between my wide-spread thighs, propped up on his elbows inches away from my stroking hand and my open, eager cunt. I want it so much that I prise open an eyelid to see if it is true. Of course it isn't, I have not heard the door or felt his weight on the bed but if

I wish hard enough I feel that the next time I open my eyes Todd will be there. I work on a special magical spell, a potion between my thighs that will pull him to me, bring him within touching distance. I stir the pot, left, right and back again. I sprinkle with my fingers spread, feeling the gentle taps of fingertips like raindrops as I add more to the enchantment. Each movement arouses me more, every little touch, accidental or purposeful encourages the flow of my juices and soon my fingers are slick and fragrant, calling out to be licked.

"You juicy slut." I hear his voice, not aloud but in my mind, it encourages me to force two of my fingers inside to fill me and coat them with my juices. "Fuck, you're so wet, you're such a dirty, nasty girl, fingering yourself so lewdly in front of a virtual stranger."

He's here, and not just as a voice in my head any more, I heard the door, felt the breeze on my open, sticky thighs. I was scared for a moment, not sure who it was or what they would make of my rounded figure openly masturbating in front of an open door but then I heard him groan and I realised who it was.

"You're so beautiful," he gasps, pressing the door closed with a reassuring 'click'. He makes me forget all anxiety about my shape, the worries that have built up over years of being called "fat" with just that one reassuring sentence. He loves my curves. He has always said I am a real woman built right for fucking.

I can't open my eyes; the need to see scares me to a point where I just freeze up. "Don't stop," he begs, "this is what I want, what I need, please, Elle. Please continue playing with that wet pussy, let me watch you."

I open my eyes and he is walking towards me. He sits on the end of the bed and smiles at me. He throws off his jacket and I continue, my fingers play around my clit and

I shudder with pleasure. I am so turned on I feel as if I might burst at any moment.

"My sweet slut," he murmurs, "you smell so good, I knew you would."

"Want a taste?" I cannot believe the ease with which I speak those words, the good girl in me blushes, my cheeks burn red but my cunt clenches and I realise that deep inside I really am very naughty.

"Yes, dear God, yes," I lean forward, and he moves towards me until his thigh brushes my toes and I hold out my hand to him. He closes his eyes and inhales deeply, the natural rouge of my cheeks deepens and I gasp as his lips enclose my fingers. His eyes flick open again and our gazes meet and meld as his lips exert more pressure. He laps my juices with moans and gasps that roll through my body making it long for the orgasm denied it so far.

"Keep playing," he urges, "I need to see more."

I move my wet fingers from his lips to my cunt and press them inside me as I watch him watching me. He shifts on the bed, I long to feel him touch me, but no, he's shifting back a little so he can see my fingers inside me clearer.

I am desperate to come now, the play, the excitement, the reality of this moment, my fantasy come true, pushes me to the very edge of my arousal. I whimper as I strum my finger over my raging clit, the desperation transferring from my hand to my pulsing pussy and I whimper as I feel the orgasm growing inside me.

"Come for me," he growls. I had barely realised I'd shut my eyes till that moment when they flicked open again and I see him focusing on my fingers, his hand cradling his crotch through the straining material of his trousers.

I want him, I need him, but I cannot stop myself now,

the orgasm grows and blooms my fingers work hard until the internal pressure bursts and I come all over my fingers, juices streaming as I call his name.

"So sexy, so beautiful," he moans, "I want to taste more of you." I move my fingers from my still twitching cunt but he does not want the taste second-hand this time. He rolls between my thighs and starts to lick. He whirls his tongue across the top of one thigh and I sigh, delighted to feel his lips on me and aching to feel more.

I have come, I should be sated but no, with every movement of his lips on my thigh, with every lap of his tongue and stroke from his fingers I become more and yet more aroused.

"You taste so good," he says, then licks higher, "so fucking good, sweet and tangy, musky and soft. I want more."

He stops talking and starts eating at precisely the right moment and it is as if he is devouring me like a favoured meal. He starts with gentle licks that tickle and arouse my plump lips. His tongue seeks out every drop of my juice, up and down lips, under them and deeper into me. He teases me with a tongue tip, hinting at how he could fill me but retreats as if tasting hesitantly, wanting to savour the flavour and save it for the end of the meal.

He finds my clit but he is gentle with it, it is raw and throbbing with the orgasm just achieved and he knows this. His gentle tongue laps around it but never directly on it, bringing it back to arousal. Soon I feel the tension building again and I am begging him to lick my clit.

He does not rush, I have my hands in his hair and I'm pulling and twisting and pushing on his head but he stubbornly sticks to the slow licks and the teasing tempo he has already established.

It is not until I am whimpering and arching my back

with need that he shouts.

"Enough."

I freeze in place, scared by his outburst, wondering what it might mean. Slowly I open an eye as I feel his weight shift. He has lifted to his knees and he is ripping off his shirt. Button after button falls under the assault and inch by desirable inch his bare flesh comes into view. His shirt is discarded and I am still unable to move. My fingers are gripping into the bed sheets and my thighs are spread lewdly. He has not looked away from my body and is still tracing the contours of my revealed breasts as he rips down the zip on his pants and yanks his underwear down impatiently.

His cock is magnificent, hard and straining towards me, eager to feel my juicy cunt around its turgid flesh. I want to lick it, touch it, caress it and make it mine and in time, I will, I promise myself that but now I am as eager to feel him fill me as he is to be inside of me.

"Fuck me," the words fall from my lips unbidden, as if the force of my thoughts had propelled them from my body and into the air.

"Certainly," he replies with a wry smile and a cheeky wink. We laugh, connecting more in that moment than when his tongue was inside me. We are friends, fellow perverts and now lovers too.

He crawls forward, the trousers pulling lower down as he moves towards me. It takes a matter of seconds but feels like an eternity as I wait to feel him against me and inside me. "I've waited so long," he says as he positions himself between my curvy thighs, "I am going to fuck you hard and fast, my love, I do not believe I could manage anything else right now."

"Good," I reply, looking directly back at him, "I need a good hard fucking from you."

He growls and pushes forward. We are still joined by our gazes as he pushes his cock against my spread lips. We look into each other's eyes as his cock finds my entrance and presses in. The head pierces me and the shaft follows smoothly, filling me and pushing out moans of pure unabashed pleasure from between my lips.

"You feel so good," he gasps as he pulls back, his eyes still locked upon me, "your cunt is wetter, hotter, juicer than I've ever imagined, fuck, it's perfect."

I had never had a man wax lyrical about the features of my pussy before but I enjoy it and my cunt clenches around him in a show of appreciation for his kind words and his thick cock stretching me.

He closes his eyes as he rocks his hips forward and back creating a rhythm. I push up with my hips to meet him. I need the pressure now and the impact of pelvis against pelvis. His pace quickens and he bends over, resting his weight on his arms on either side of my shoulders.

He uses the extra grip to thrust even harder into me and I yelp with the pleasure of his cock pistoning in and out of me. It is hard and fast and I am quickly approaching orgasm.

"Fuck yes," I cry, overwhelmed by the ecstasy caused by his movements, I reach round and grab on to him, my fingers dig into his back and I cling on wanting to feel more of his body against mine as we career along the tracks to orgasm. He powers on, his eyes flick open and our lips reach for each other and the brief kiss leaves my lips tingling.

My eyes close as I feel the tightening of my pussy and the aching of my clit, which can mean only one thing,

"Fuck, I'm gonna come," I gasp, overcome by the overwhelming need to share the obvious.

"Yes, come on my cock, you dirty slut, come all over me, I'm going to fill you, fuck yes, squeeze me, make me come."

I follow his instructions to the letter. I yelp and dig my nails into his flesh as my pussy squeezes hard and the pleasure explodes through my body. I scream, unable to hold in the immense force of ecstasy ripping through me and as the scream peters out I hear his roar as his cock thickens and pulses inside me.

"Hi," he says, a grin stretched across his warm pink face.

"Hey," I giggle back as he leans in and kisses me, "how are you?"

"I am pretty damn good," he replies, rolling to the side of me and pressing his body close, "you?"

"Fantastic," I purr, "now you're here."

"I told you we'd make it happen, didn't I?"

"Yes." I roll slightly to the side and he wraps an arm around me, pulling me close to him, "I didn't believe it ever would, it seemed so complicated."

"Not now, it's simple. I'm here, you're here and fuck you're hot."

"I could say the same of you," I chuckle, "but it'll give you a big head."

"Mmm, I thought you enjoyed my big head." He squeezes my thigh and lets out a hearty chuckle.

"Yes, yes I did." My cheeks flush red with embarrassment, which seems awfully silly considering just how intimate we've just been. "How was the journey?" I asked, simply to fill the silence.

"Oh, not so bad, thanks. I wish it had been a little quicker so I could have seen more of your show."

"I think you saw quite a lot of it anyway," I run my hand down his chest, enjoying the warm hardness of it beneath my fingers.

"I could never get enough of you, sweetheart, you're addictive, I want more and more and more of your abundance."

"Oh good, because I feel exactly the same way about you." I beam back and lean over to kiss him, my hand skimming over his stomach and belly button as my lips meet his. They come together with such force that it sends shockwaves through my body and excites my cunt once more. The deft movements of his lips beneath mine and gentle press of his tongue into my mouth is a thing of sheer erotic beauty and I can barely move as he kisses me with such passionate precision.

I recover my senses and kiss back and my hand moves lower as if on autopilot. I skim over the top of his pubis and then dart to the left, he moans as I slip down over his hip and I caress his thigh, my fingers creeping slowly over the warm stickiness of his inner thigh. I can feel my juices there as I swirl my fingers around in a twirl and catch the side of his tightening balls.

I suck the moan from his mouth to mine and my fingers climb over on to his soft and giving balls. The skin crinkles like velvet under my touch. I can feel my sticky juices coating him still, it reminds me of the fucking he just gave me and flares my arousal once more. I kiss harder and cup his balls in my hand. He moans and presses into the warmth of my giving body, his tongue probing my mouth lewdly, making me long to be filled completely.

I move my hand higher and brush the base of his cock, it is hard and straining already and I have to wrap my hand around it, I cannot resist a moment longer. The weight is satisfying as I squeeze gently and sweep my fist up to the pinnacle and slide it back down again. He is hot and sticky in my hand, hard and unyielding. I break our kiss so I can look down and enjoy the view.

I watch in a hypnotic trance as his cock hides in my fist then reveals itself to me over and over as I pump up and down. Todd moans and hisses with pleasure and I revel in the power I have over him, the power of arousal. I would love to tease him until he anoints my fingers with his come but I am impatient and my cunt is hungry once more.

"Lie back, baby." I whisper as I move on to my knees. He scooches down on to his back and moves into the middle of the bed as I shift over to accommodate him. I pull the satin away from my body as it wraps itself around my legs. He groans and reaches out to cup and mould my soft naked breasts in his hands.

Once he is flat I swing my leg across his body and position myself above his straining dick. I reach between my thighs and grab it. Gently I press it to my wet hole and enjoy the hiss of breath through his clenched teeth as I ease him inside me.

I love to push down and fill my hungry cunt with hard, hot cock. The power of controlling the speed and thrust is delicious and as I push up and down I arch my back and moan out my pleasure.

I hear a click but ignore it, too wrapped up in what I'm doing, but I notice Todd look slightly left of me and smile. He has his hands on my hips and he's crooning now, encouraging me on with noises that stir my emotions and fuel my lusts.

"You're so beautiful,' he growls as I cup my breasts and stretch my fingers round to tease my nipples. I am watching him now as he talks, meeting his gaze and revelling in his words. "That's it, fuck me, take my cock deeper into that hot, wet cunt." He digs his fingers into my soft hips and I yelp with shock and arousal. "My sweet slut," he continues, "ride me, make me come."

"Yes," I moan, "fill me, fucking fill me." My cunt squeezes and I feel his hard cock throb within me.

"Oh, Elle," he groans and squeezes me again. My eyes had closed in pleasure but they flick open to see him looking to the left again. I knot my brow and he notices then mouths, 'we are being watched,' and my pussy pulses again.

We have someone watching us. Some man or woman is standing at the door watching my big arse rise up and down. With each lift that person will see my pussy lips wrapped around his thick member and will watch my cunt swallow it every time I sink down its length to the very root.

I slow things down now, wanting to give our voyeur a show, Todd grins as he realises what I am doing and his hands move off my hips. He uses one finger to beckon me closer. I bend at the waist and rest myself on my hands. He whispers in my ear, "You like being watched, don't you, slut?"

I nod my head as my hips continue to rise and fall.

"I know, I can feel the juices dripping around my cock and your cunt squeezing me in pleasure. You're putting on a show aren't you, dirty girl?"

I nod again and he captures my lips with his. His hands move down my back to my arse and as we kiss hard and lustfully he grabs my buttocks, one in each hand. Gently he pulls and I know he is displaying more of my cunt to the gaze of our onlooker. He is displaying his sex in mine and allowing the voyeur a closer look at our lovemaking. I tingle and shake with arousal as I imagine what the person at the door can see. I am almost jealous but I realise that I prefer actually fucking to watching.

He digs his fingers into my bum and his hips begin to thrust. I can tell he is close to orgasm as he desperately thrusts up into me.

"Come for me," I moan as I intensify my thrusts to satisfy his desperation, "fill my hot, slutty cunt. Give me your cum, fill me, up I need your cum." I babble and moan louder and louder as his arousal transfers from his pounding cock to my aching, sensitive clit.

"Yes," he groans as he stiffens, I feel his cock clench and relax inside of me as my plump pussy pulses and the pleasure shakes my whole body. I slide down and envelope him inside me as he expands and contracts, the last shots of pleasure flowing from him to me.

"Wow," I whisper as I disengage and fall to the bed beside him, "that was so good."

"Mmm," he replies, too blissed out to say more. We hear another faint click and when we look up, the door is closed again.

"I thought you were a voyeur," I tease, snuggling into Todd's warm, replete body.

"Seems I'm an exhibitionist when I'm with you, too. I want to show you off, baby, you're so good."

I blush and giggle. It's good to experience both sides of the coin, maybe next time I'll get to be the voyeur.

The Photographer's Muse
by Scarlett Sanderson

Cathy bit down on her lip. Anticipation coursed through her body, settling in the pit of her stomach. She stared at her reflection in the mirror. Today was the first day of her new beginning. Out with the old Cathy, in with the new.

Yeah, right.

She unbuttoned her shirt. If this was a good idea, why were her hands shaking?

Replying to a 'Curvy Model Wanted' ad in the local news seemed like a good idea at the time. Now she wasn't so sure.

The model was expected to pose in a very scanty piece of lingerie. Her gaze drifted to the black velvet effect box. Inside lay a scarlet lace overlay bustier complete with G-string and stockings. Cathy swallowed. She'd never worn anything so revealing … or so sexy. She'd always been self-conscious of her curves. She'd never been bold enough to wear the sexy lingerie most women did.

Lifting the lid off the box, she took out the bustier. The fabric felt wonderful against her fingers. She wondered what it would feel like against her skin. A wicked image of her dressed in the scarlet outfit, wearing a pair of shocking red high heels and wielding a feather whip, flashed through her mind. It wasn't an unpleasant thought. In fact, it thrilled her, sent ribbons of desire coursing through her body. She fingered the satin and lace, rubbing it between her thumb and forefinger. So soft. So slippery. Like the feel of a man's cock in the wet cavern of her mouth.

A knock at the door broke her thoughts. "Cathy? Are you nearly done?"

Rachel was the photographer's assistant. She'd vetted the applicants and chosen the 'winner'. Cathy had yet to meet James Seymour. With a name like James, she expected a crusty, old guy. Or a gay one.

"I'm nearly done, I'll be right out."

Swallowing her fear, putting aside her doubts, Cathy lifted her head, took a deep breath and stripped off. Stepping into the bustier was easy. The closing of the hook eyes at the back proved more difficult. She struggled, but after a few tries managed to get them clasped. After pulling on the G-string and attaching the stockings, she glanced at herself in the mirror.

Wow.

She looked ... sexy. Her full breasts spilled out of the cups in an enticing way. The dusky pink tips of her nipples were visible through the scraps of lace. Her waist tapered then flared. Her curvy thighs looked luscious in the red garters. The transformation was extraordinary. She'd never known a piece of lingerie could make her feel so special.

She tugged on a robe. Time to meet her photographer.

Opening the door, she peeked out and gave Rachel a shy smile. "I'm ready."

"That's great." The assistant ushered her out through a set of doors and into a studio flooded with light. "James is all set up and ready to go."

Rachel pointed at the figure with his back facing them. Cathy gulped. From the back, the view was delicious. The figure wore a tight white T-shirt and faded jeans. Broad, muscular shoulders filled out the T-shirt to perfection. The jeans encased an ass so perfect Cathy resisted the urge to bite down on a closed fist.

His bare feet caught and held her attention. How very bohemian.

He's got to be gay.

"James, your model's here. This is Cathy."

When he turned, Cathy retracted her preconceived notion about his sexuality. This was a man who loved women. His dark, messy hair stood out in all directions, as if he constantly ran his hand through it. There was a wicked glint in his green eyes, a glint suggesting he was pure Alpha male.

She gulped. Did that make her prey?

Dear God, she hoped so!

His chiselled face showcased perfectly sculpted lips and slashed eyebrows. Handsome and sexy in a manly, dangerous way. When he smiled, Cathy felt as if she would melt into a pool of orgasmic harmony. Her body responded instantly. Her pussy became wet, readying her for the hefty bulge she noted at the front of his pants.

"Hi, Cathy." He held out his hand. "Pleased to meet you. Thanks for agreeing to model for me today."

She blushed and chided herself for her schoolgirl indulgence. She was a woman. A liberated, strong woman who wasn't afraid to get semi naked in front of a gorgeous stranger.

Pfftttt!

"Shall we begin?" James's voice held a slight Irish lilt.

Damn, she'd always been a sucker for an Irish accent.

Pushing her wicked thoughts aside, Cathy nodded. "Where do you want me?"

His gaze snapped to hers. Heat blazed in his eyes.

She blinked. Her cheeks heated with a blush as she

thought about the double meaning. She knew exactly where she wanted to be – on her back, legs splayed in the air with James pounding his cock into her. Either that or on her knees sucking his cock into her mouth, teasing him to the point of distraction.

"Over here." He motioned to a boudoir seat and she was reminded of numerous burlesque settings she'd seen in photographs.

Once she was seated, he pointed at her robe. "Take that off, please."

Crunch time. Slipping the robe off, she shook it to the ground. Her gaze moved everywhere except to James. She found she couldn't meet his gaze, yet she was dying to see the reaction on his face.

His sharp intake of breath finally made her look in his direction. If she'd thought his eyes burned passionately before, she'd been wrong. The green orbs were now aflame with unmistakable desire. His gaze raked over her curves with a hungry sweep of possession. Remembering his professionalism, James shook his head slightly, as if dispelling some form of trance.

"Perfect."

They spent a few minutes in silence. James rearranged her body to exactly the position he wanted. His warm hands skimmed over her curves. Her nipples became throbbing peaks against the lace and she prayed he didn't notice. If he did she could always blame it on the cool air.

The heated grin he gave her squashed the notion. Of course he'd noted her reaction to his hands. He took photographs for a living; it was his job to *see*.

"Now," he picked up a camera, "I want you to look at me. Look into the lens and imagine you're looking at a lover. Imagine you've taken the time to set this up. You're planning to seduce me. Give me a seductive look."

She gave him her best come-hither look. He snapped a few shots then shook his head.

"Nope, something is not quite right ..."

Laying down the camera, he once again raked his gaze over her body. His eyes blazed with heat. He followed the shape of her curves with his hand. As she watched his hand move against the air, Cathy's mouth went dry. Her eyelids fluttered closed for just a moment as she imagined him running that hand across her body, feeling his heat through the lace of the bustier, cupping her tits, spilling them into his hands and tweaking her nipples until she moaned with pleasure. She licked her lips in anticipation, squeezed her thighs together as her cunt gushed ...

"Right there! That's it! Don't move! Perfect!" She heard the shutter of his camera click repeatedly.

Opening her eyes, she looked at him through hooded lids.

"You're Venus. A goddess. A siren sent to tempt men to do wicked things. A wanton woman ..." All the while he spoke his camera buzzed.

She threw back her head and laughed at his words. His exuberance was infectious.

"Jesus, Cathy, that's perfect!"

Enjoying herself, Cathy slipped into the moment. She forgot the setting; instead, she fantasised about James. She imagined he really was her lover, that the pictures he took were for his personal collection. Luxuriating in the attention, she ran her hands seductively over her curves. First her breasts, then down over her curved stomach to her thighs. Her hands idled so close to her pussy, she could feel the heat emanating in waves. Her clit throbbed in time with her pulse. She wanted to slip her fingers inside the seams of her G-string and rub her clit. She was so turned on. She couldn't believe she was acting so bold, feeling so fucking sexy.

The silence made her glance at James. He'd stopped taking photographs. Instead he stared at her, mouth slightly agape, eyes blazing with heat.

Good lord, he was gorgeous! And from the look on his face he thought the same about her.

Giving him a wicked grin, she crooked a finger in his direction. Inviting him. Enticing him. Cathy didn't know what had gotten into her. Maybe it was the situation. Maybe it was James's wicked green eyes, or maybe it was the lingerie …

She did exactly what she'd been fantasising about. Slipping her fingers inside the hem of the G-string, she kept her gaze locked on James. As she rubbed her fingertips up and down the satin, pulling the fabric away from her pulsing cunt, giving him teasing glances of her wet pussy, she watched his nostrils flare. The fabric of his jeans pulled tight across his groin and she could see the outline of his impressive cock as it hardened.

He took a step towards her and she shook her head.

"No, stay there. I want you to watch. You're the photographer, the artist."

He didn't answer her, but he didn't move either. Instead he stood transfixed, mesmerised by the movement of her fingers. The look of rapture on his face made Cathy bolder. Her clit beat at a thumping pace; she felt it harden, peak from the fleshy hood. Biting her lip, she swept a fingertip over her clit, gave the nub a slow, leisurely rub, circled her finger around and around. Unable to resist, she dipped her fingers into her pussy, pumping a few times. When her fingers were slick enough, she pulled out and raised them to her lips. Her tongue snaked out and she lapped at the warm honey from her cunt.

James groaned. He fisted one of his hands before lifting up his camera and snapping off a picture.

Cathy grinned seductively. Every nerve ending in her body pulsed with electricity. In a matter of hours she'd gone from being a plus-size 'model to be' to a porn star. Maybe she'd always had this inside her – a repressed sexual side. Right now she didn't give a fuck. She didn't have the motor functions to overanalyse. What she wanted was to come and for James to watch.

With more authority than she thought possible, Cathy spoke: "I'm going to come now, James, and you are going to watch me as I finger my pussy. I'm going to come all over my fingers and I want you to imagine it's your cock getting me off. Can you do that, James?"

His eyes blazed. His cock jerked in his jeans. "Come for me, Cathy. Now. Make your pussy cream."

She moaned at his words. Her clit beat wildly like someone drumming fingertips on her mound. Throwing back her head, she pushed the G-string aside and shoved three fingers inside her pussy. As she pumped them in and out, in and out, she lifted her legs up and parted her thighs wide enough to penetrate deeper. It felt so good to be fingering herself.

"That's it, Cathy, fuck your cunt." His whispered words of encouragement were accompanied by sounds of a camera clicking.

She didn't care. All that mattered was reaching orgasm.

Sliding her thumb over her pubic bone, she pressed down on her clit, rubbing it in vigorous circles against the bone. Biting her lip, she concentrated on the fantasy in her mind. In this reality James unbuttoned his fly and fisted his hard cock in his hand, running his palm up and down the rigid length, pushing back foreskin to reveal a bulbous purple head. After a few pulls he threw back his head and spurted hot sticky cum all over her generous tits ...

Unable to hold back, Cathy sped up the vibrations on her clit. The image of James coming on her curves was enough to send her over the edge. Her orgasm ripped through her, leaving her panting and sated. Slumping back on the couch she rearranged the G-string to cover her soaking cunt. Leaning back, she focused on breathing at a normal rate.

The tingling sensation in her body alerted her that someone was close by. Opening her eyes slowly, she saw James standing over her. His camera hung limply at his side. Her gaze roamed to his groin. His cock looked painfully hard, straining against the metal zipper.

Licking her lips, Cathy gave him her best seductive smile and wiggled her eyebrows.

James laughed.

It broke some of the erotic tension in the air.

"Ahem!" A quiet cough from the corner of the room brought Cathy crashing back to reality. She met Rachel's amused smile and her cheeks flared with heated embarrassment. "I think I should leave."

James put down his camera. "No need, Rae. I think we are done here."

Deflated and embarrassed at her forwardness, Cathy slipped into her robe. "I guess I'll be getting dressed."

Fumbling to tie the sash, she watched Rachel take the roll of film offered by James as he cleared away his equipment.

"Gonna get this to the lab. See you again, Cathy." With a friendly wave, she was gone.

They were left alone. The photographer and his muse.
Well, this is awkward.
"Will you be needing me again?"

James looked up and tilted his head to the side. His gaze met hers before travelling down her body.

A slow, easy smile formed on his lips. "I'll always be needing you, Cathy. You're my muse." He leaned over and tucked a stray strand of hair behind her ear. "How about I take you to dinner? To say thanks."

Cathy returned his smile. "I'd love to, but let me get out of this outfit first."

The hot look James gave her heated her blood to boiling point.

"OK, but you might be needing it later."

Meeting My Husband Again
by Deva Shore

I was nervous. It had been nearly two years since I'd seen my husband, and a lot had happened since. As I stood at the dock waiting for his ship to come in I thought back to the last time I'd stood here – only that time I was waving him goodbye.

'I wish I could be here with you when the baby comes,' he'd said.

'So do I, darling. But we can't change the war, can we?' I'd wept.

'I'll miss you,' he said, looking deeply into my eyes.

'Me too. Be careful,' I said tearfully into his neck, as his hand came around to pat my stomach.

'Who knows,' he chuckled, 'maybe you'll get those breasts you've always wanted when the baby's born.'

We kissed passionately as I clung to him, praying this wouldn't be the last time we'd see each other.

I got those breasts and more. I went from a size ten, with small breasts, hips and thighs, to a large eighteen. I'd grown all over and I was terrified he wouldn't love me any more.

We'd had an amazing sex life. John was always randy. Loved sex and showing me off. Whenever we went out he loved nothing more than to see me in a super-mini skirt, bare midriff and tight T-shirt. He loved guys whistling at me and said there was nothing wrong with them looking as long as they didn't touch.

All my friends were jealous of my stick-like figure but me, well, I would have preferred bigger breasts and more rounded hips. I'd looked at my friends enviously, wishing desperately for their curves, finding it ironic that we were never happy with what we had.

But now I was. I had no intention of losing any weight. I felt sexy and alive, never more feminine. I only hoped John would feel the same. So it was with shaky legs that I stood there waiting, hoping I'd get the reaction I longed for.

All the photos I'd sent to John had been mainly of Charlotte, our daughter. I made sure that any that included me were the most flattering. My stomach fluttered as he walked slowly down the plank, his eyes searching everywhere for me.

He glanced my way and I lifted my hand. He continued to search for me and my mouth went dry. I licked my lips nervously. What if he didn't like the changes in me? As he continued to search the crowd, I made my way over to the plank. Happiness was everywhere: women were crying, laughing; men were spinning their wives off their feet and whisking children in the air, happy to be reunited once again.

Finally John's eyes swept over me. He didn't smile at first and my heart dropped. Was he disappointed in how I looked? I threw my arms around his neck and then put Charlotte into his arms.

'God, it's been so long,' I said.

'Yes. Oh, God, she's beautiful,' he said as he lifted her proudly and showed her off to all his friends.

'I missed you,' I said.

'I missed you more,' he said, putting his arm around me.

His fingers lingered on my love handles. Then his hand roamed down over my hip where it stayed possessively. I pointed out our car and together we moved forwards, a family reunited.

John strapped Charlotte into her car seat and I sat behind the steering wheel.

'You look great,' he said after the ignition roared to life.

'You sure? You're not disappointed I haven't lost all the weight I put on after having Charlotte?'

'No, not at all. In fact, you look amazing. Absolutely stunning.'

'Really?'

'Yes, really! I always thought you were too skinny before,' he laughed.

'Why didn't you tell me?'

'Who can tell a woman anything? I was worried if I told you you'd get all paranoid and think I didn't love you.'

Was he just saying that? I hated feeling so insecure. We'd always had such a great sex life and I was terrified he'd be repulsed by my weight. I'd gone out and bought a sexy teddy, one that actually fit. It was red. His favourite colour. With a plunging neckline, it was so low that my nipples peeked out over the top. My areolas had grown so large, they had darkened in colour and my nipples were huge from having breastfed.

We chatted all the way home as I brought him up to date with what had passed since he'd left. As I drove up the driveway, I felt relieved to finally have him home.

'Everything looks great,' he said. 'You've done a brilliant job since I've been gone.'

'Thanks, darling,' I said as his hand found its way between my thighs.

'Hmm, feels nice,' he said, inching his fingers further.

'Not now,' I said looking back at Charlotte, who was gurgling happily in her car seat.

'Yes, now. As soon as I get you in that front door I'm going to make love to you like never before.'

'I can hardly wait,' I giggled.

I'd organised a surprise party, so when he opened the door all our family and friends let out a welcome he'd never forget. He looked at me and I him, knowing full well that making love would now have to wait. The party was wonderful. He was happy to catch up with everyone and when they all finally left and we were alone, he pulled me into his arms.

'Thanks for the party but what I really wanted was to be alone with you,' he said, looking down into my flushed face. 'You look radiant.'

I blushed further, feeling like a new bride, as though tonight was our first time. I must admit I was very nervous. We put Charlotte to bed and while I packed the dishwasher, John had a shower. He snuck up behind me wearing only a towel. His hands reached out to squeeze my breasts.

'Hmm,' he mumbled into my neck, 'nice, very nice.'

I pushed my arse back into him, loving his hands on me.

'Go and have a shower,' he insisted, slapping me on the bum. 'I'll finish up here.'

I turned in his arms and kissed him, and all the old feelings came flooding back tenfold.

Walking towards our bedroom, I looked back over my shoulder and saw him watching me. I hoped he wouldn't be disappointed.

I grabbed the teddy, red suspender and black fishnet stockings and locked myself in the bathroom. Taking off my clothes I eyed myself in the mirror. My hands roamed over my voluptuous breasts. I lifted them as though offering them, pleased with the way they looked. I loved the feel of them, their fullness. They made me feel so sexy. I didn't want to be skinny again. I loved being this weight, loved feeling the thickness of my waist and the way my hands slid over my body.

I loved the way my thighs rubbed together as I walked. After a heavy night of masturbating, when my pussy lips were swollen and protruding, I loved nothing more than to feel the sensation there, the thickness of my thighs causing vibrations to ripple through my clit.

I opened the shower door and hit the taps, turning the water on full blast. Stepping in, I allowed the water to wash away any tension I was feeling. I soaped myself up, my hands slipping over my wet body. I reached down towards my pussy, my fingers running through my pubic hair. God, that felt good, but it felt even better when I parted the folds and allowed my fingers to slip in and out before flicking over my clit.

The water cascaded down, easing the tension and heightening my desire. I turned to face the nozzle, allowing it to sting my breasts, the nipples hardening under the force. I'd waited a long time for John to come home. The vibrators and dildos I'd purchased while he was away were nowhere near as good as the real thing, so I quickly turned off the taps, enveloped myself in a large bath sheet and patted myself dry.

I carefully applied just a small amount of make-up, wanting to look as sexy as possible without going over the top. I smeared on some red lipstick, the same shade as the teddy, before squeezing myself into my outfit.

I glimpsed my reflection as I hooked the fishnets into the garter. I was bending over and my breasts were practically spilling out. I thought I looked great, but would John? Standing back, I turned around, wanting to see how my arse looked. My hips and cheeks were curvaceous, in proportion to my breasts. I'd certainly changed from the way I used to look. I slipped my arms into a matching robe and slid my feet into stilettos, and then made my entrance. I strode as purposefully into the bedroom as a panther would stalk its prey.

'Oh God, Melissa, you look fucking gorgeous,' John said, wolf-whistling as I advanced upon him.

He was lying in the centre of the bed, the towel still attached, his arms behind his head. I yanked the towel from him and threw it on to the floor. His cock was semi flaccid, lying over his groin. I looked from it to him before I jumped on the bed, picked it up and held it just inches away from my red-painted lips. I breathed on it, my breath hot as my tongue stole its way forward to lick it.

'Oh yeah,' John said, staring at me. 'I've been waiting so long for that.'

Sucking the knob into my mouth, I rolled it around my tongue, enjoying the taste and feel of him. It had been so long since I had the real thing. I wanted to straddle him and fuck his brains out, but on the other hand I wanted to make it last, wanted this first night of the new me to be one I never forgot, so instead I sucked a bit harder, pleased when I heard his appreciative moan.

'Oh baby, that feels so good,' he murmured.

My hand began to pump his shaft. He stiffened quickly, his cock throbbing in my palm. Eager to please him, I decided it might be better to have him come first, and then he could spend more time with foreplay for me, but that wasn't what John wanted. Instead, he gently disengaged himself from me.

'I've been dreaming of this night for so long,' he said.

He rose, pulled me up into his arms, and we kissed passionately. I could hardly breathe, I was so turned on. I slipped my robe down over my shoulders and it fell in a heap at my feet. John pulled away from me, kept me at arm's length, his eyes boring into me as he soaked in my new body.

His fingers trailed down over the swell of my breasts, causing goosebumps to break out on my skin. He lowered his head, his lips grazing where his fingers had just been. He then ran them down the inside of my waist, over my hips and to the top of the stockings.

'Beautiful,' he said as his fingers played with the tops of the stocking, inching their way underneath a fraction to nip the skin. 'You look so beautiful.'

I was breathing heavily, my breasts rising and falling against the front of the teddy, the nipples now showing just a fraction more, straining hard against the flimsy material.

John lay me down on the bed, sat on the side, his cock rigid before him. I made to grab for it but he slapped my hand away. Lifting both my hands, he held them above my head as he straddled me. He then ran his fingers down my arms, over my breasts to my waist and then back to linger at the plunging neckline.

I was trembling all over as his eyes swept over me wolfishly. He grabbed my tits, squeezing them through the material before coming up to kiss my mouth. I could barely stand it. I wanted him to ravish me, fuck me quickly, stop making me wait and do what I'd been dreaming of for so long.

Now his hands were digging inside the teddy and he lifted my breasts out. Smothering his face into my cleavage he kissed each breast in turn, giving both the same amount of attention. When his mouth began to suckle me I squirmed beneath him, my hands coming down to hold his head.

'Oh, baby,' I said. 'I love you.'

A hand was moving downwards between us, and I opened my legs for him. He ran over my mound, his fingers plucking at the material over my crutch. I held him firmer, whimpering as he played with that soft, fleshy part of skin on my thighs.

'Please, make love to me,' I begged.

He rose above me, looking down at me, his eyes saying so much. He grabbed at the front of the teddy, pulling the material together, and then with one quick yank he ripped it clean off my body.

I gasped excitedly as I lay there, nearly naked for his eyes to feast on.

'Oh God, your tits,' he said, caressing them, 'are so fucking gorgeous. I never dreamed you could look this great.'

I giggled as he smothered himself into them, massaging, licking and nibbling at my nipples. My pussy throbbed, eager for some attention of its own. I squirmed beneath him, trying to encourage him down. Trailing kisses from my breasts all the way down to my pussy, he lay between my open thighs, his eyes peeking over my mound mischievously.

'Open them wider,' he said.

Willingly I did. He nuzzled in and my legs closed around his head on instinct. He murmured his approval as his fingers opened my pussy lips, gently, like he was opening a petal of flowers.

'You smell fantastic,' he said, licking at my lips.

'Fuck me, baby,' I begged.

Now he was licking at my slit, his tongue tantalising

me before finding the nub of my clit. My juices were flowing out of me. It took all my willpower not to wrestle him over and fuck his brains out.

Then he tormented me further by nipping the flesh at the top of the inside of my thighs while his hand stole inside the fishnet stocking. He fumbled with the garters, undoing them and pushing the stocking down to leave it dangling at my ankle. I opened my leg for him and he kissed his way down to my foot.

Fiddling with the strap of my stiletto, he undid the shoe and threw it to the floor. He kissed the instep of my foot, and I thought I'd pass out from lust. I was wild for him, wild for him to make love to me.

It was sheer torture to lie there before him, and when he began to work his way back up I wrapped my other leg around his back, kicked his cheek with the heel of my shoe and guided him to me. His cock probed around my pussy lips and my hand quickly grabbed hold of his shaft, steering him into my hot, wet cunt. He pulled back a bit but I was determined now and thrust myself upwards. His cock sunk inside me and the moment was magical.

John was like a new man. He began to fuck me rhythmically, grabbing at my breasts, kissing them, smothering his face into my cleavage while I held on to his head, not wanting him to stop.

He rolled me over on top of him, clutching at me with his hands.

'Melissa, you're driving me wild. I've never felt so horny in my life,' he said, his fingers grabbing at my hips, my arse.

He held on to me while I slammed myself down, impaling myself on his cock. My tits were jiggling all over the place. His hands were all over me.

'I can't get enough of you,' he said. 'Fuck, I love you.'

'I love you too, baby,' I screamed as an orgasm gushed from me.

He thrust himself upwards. Perspiration dripped from both of us as he came, deep inside me, shuddering and gasping. When he'd finally calmed down I rolled off him and snuggled up against him.

'Don't you ever change,' he said.

'You really like me like this?'

'No, baby, I love you. Love you more than you'll ever know. You've never looked sexier,' he said, stroking my breast and causing the nipple to harden.

My fingers curled around his flaccid cock, then down over his balls where I gave them a gentle squeeze. Stroking his shaft gently, I felt it begin to throb. I quickly glanced at his handsome face and he chuckled deep in his throat.

'I told you baby, you've never looked sexier and I'll never be able to get enough of you,' he said.

'Welcome home,' I said as my mouth covered his amazing cock.

Fashionably Late
by Heidi Champa

'Do these pants make me look fat?'

I heard him sigh from across the room. I couldn't help asking. Even though I knew he hated it, I asked anyway. Nothing I had tried on was working for me. I unzipped the pants before he even answered me and threw them into the pile of discarded clothes. He turned around and looked at me, his hands frozen on the buttons of his shirt.

'You aren't serious, Sarah, are you? How many times have I told you to stop doing that? You look great. Put on those black pants that you had on first and let's go downstairs. The guests will be arriving any minute.'

I looked at myself in the mirror. James was just trying to placate me. I slid my hands over my thick thighs and hips. Even in the black pants, my most flattering pair, my lumps and bumps were clearly visible. He was being kind, because he loved me. And, of course, he still looked amazing after all these years. I, on the other hand, had slowly packed on the pounds. Despite my best efforts, the extra weight was impossible to hide. James caught me staring at my flaws in the mirror and walked towards me. His eyes shone with a mix of frustration and anger. I hadn't seen that look in a while.

'Stop it, Sarah. Stop tearing yourself down. I'm not going to let you do this any more. What is it going to take to make you believe that you are beautiful?'

I just shook my head at his nice words. He may have thought of me as beautiful, but I didn't. I tried to turn back to the mirror, but James stopped me.

'I see I'm going to have to get tough with you. Maybe you need to be punished for being so mean to yourself. Is that what you want, Sarah? Do you want me to punish you?'

Before I could answer, James pulled me to him. His body pressed me into the old wooden door, the mirror cool on my back. His knee settled between my legs, pushing up between my thighs. I could feel his hard cock resting against my belly, his breath hot in my ear. James slid his tongue over my neck, capturing my earlobe in his hot mouth. He flicked open my bra, rubbing his hands roughly over my full breasts. He certainly loved my new, bigger tits. Honestly, so did I. It was the only perk of weight gain.

All I was left wearing now was my new, bigger version of sexy panties. I hated them, but he loved the black, silky French-cut briefs as much as he loved my tiny thongs from our college days. Before I realised it, I was lying on the bed.

James undid his tie, the one I had given him three years before for his birthday. He grabbed my wrists and pulled them towards the wrought-iron bed frame. I didn't resist him. I couldn't have. He tied my hands tightly to the cool metal, his face hovering close to mine. He was close enough to kiss, his lips almost grazing my skin. But, as I struggled to reach his lips, he pulled back with a sly smile. His fingers grazed over my skin, lazily tracing over my soft stomach and breasts. My skin was responding to his touch, just like always. But, the edge in his eyes, the tough exterior he put on, was making me crazy. I could feel my pussy growing wetter as I awaited my fate. I made one last effort to kiss him, but he just laughed.

'I don't think so. I told you. This is your punishment. I'm going to make you see how beautiful you are. You need to be taught a lesson. So, you are going to stay here and think about what you did. Don't worry. I'll be back.'

With that, he turned and walked out of the door, locking it behind him. As I struggled against the silk, I felt my pussy tighten. A fresh wash of moisture coated my lips. The cool air from the old, drafty window caressed me, causing my nipples to harden. I heard the doorbell ring, our first guests arriving to our party. Lord knows what James would tell them about where I was. All I could do was wait for him to come back and untie me. A few minutes turned into half an hour. I could tell the party was in full swing. The voices were growing louder, the music had begun and I was beginning to wonder what kind of punishment this was.

I knew that James meant well, and that it was wrong to hate myself for my weight. But, I never realised how much it bothered him. He would roll his eyes at me when I would lament how fat I was, and no matter how much he reassured me, I still felt ugly. Especially when I saw him talking to more attractive women. I could just see him downstairs right now, flirting with his hot co-workers and fawning over our new, sexy neighbour. I was starting to get angry, but it did nothing to quell the heat between my legs.

I was beginning to think James was never coming back. It was growing more and more uncomfortable in the room. I was cold; my toes and fingers were completely numb. Despite my restless pussy, all I could think about at the moment was the nice hot tea I could get downstairs. The party sounded like it was dying down. I had no idea how much time had passed. I heard the door lock click, and saw James enter the room. My whole body relaxed as he approached the bed. He sat down next to me, the mattress bowing under his weight.

'Don't worry, I told everyone you had to go to your mother's. Last-minute emergency. Everyone sends their love. So did you miss me?'

As he asked the question, his fingers traced over my stomach, teasing down to my pussy. I was sure he could feel the heat there without even touching me. He kept going, sliding a single finger between my slick lips, stopping just above my clit.

'What do you think, James? I'm cold. And, I'm tired. Are you going to untie me or what?'

'Not until you tell me what I want to hear.'

I opened my mouth to tell him where he could shove his punishment, but he covered my lips with his, his tongue probing deeply into my mouth. His finger left my cunt and moved up to my hard nipples. He moistened each one with his damp finger, the cool air making them even harder.

'So, are you ready to say it yet, Sarah?'

'Say what?'

'That you are a beautiful woman. And, I want you to promise me you won't put yourself down any more. Your body is amazing. I'm going to prove it to you tonight.'

'I promise, Jake. I promise. Now untie me.'

As I answered, he sucked one taut nipple into his mouth. The heat was overwhelming, a stark contrast to the cool room. He sucked hard, grazing his teeth over my hard flesh without actually biting down. He toyed with the other nipple, his fingers teasing while his mouth tortured. I bucked my hips towards him, inviting him to touch me.

But, he ignored my silent pleas and continued his lazy teasing of my nipples.

He got up from the bed to shed his shirt and pants. I watched as he stood naked, his cock rising in the darkness. I was desperate to have him, and he knew it. He was going to make me wait. He sat down again, his hip resting next to mine. I waited for his next move, but he just looked at me, devouring me with his eyes.

'Is that all you have to say?'

'I told you, I promise. Now let me go.'

'There was more. You are beautiful, and I want to hear you say it.'

His finger slid over my wet lips, then all the way inside me, his palm rubbing gently over my hard clit. I tried to rub myself against him harder, but he kept pulling away from me. I moaned in disappointment as he smiled, enjoying my plight.

'I want to hear you admit it. Admit you are a beautiful woman, no matter what size you are. I love you, Sarah. And, I think you are the hottest fucking woman I've ever seen.'

I couldn't answer. I was too focused on his finger teasing me, his words hitting me like a ton of bricks.

'Come on, Sarah, say it.'

His one finger became two, pressing me open further. I cried out, squeezing my eyes shut against the sensations.

'Open your eyes, Sarah. Look at me.'

I did as he asked, staring up into his blue eyes. Even in the dark, they were sparkling. He pulled his fingers from my cunt and brought them to my mouth, making me suck them clean. It had been so long since I tasted myself. It made me even hotter.

'Say it, Sarah.'

'James, enough. I need you to fuck me, I can't wait

any more. I want it.'

'Not good enough. But, it's a start.'

He got up and moved down the bed. He pushed my thighs wide apart, and settled between them. He opened my pussy, letting the cool air hit me. I shivered, both from the cold and the feel of his fingers on me. I felt his tongue slide up and down over my wet slit. His teasing strokes avoided my clit each time, despite my efforts to move him closer with my hips. He stayed one step ahead of me, making all my squirming worthless. Finally, he took pity on me and wrapped his lips around my clit. He sucked hard, drawing it into his mouth. His fingers were back in my cunt, working in a steady rhythm with his tongue. I was practically weeping from the pleasure, my body unable to take much more. The noises from my throat were foreign even to my ears; the sounds of pure need.

'Say it, Sarah.'

'OK. I'm beautiful. And, I look good just the way I am. Now fuck me, please, fuck me, James.'

He moved up next to me again, letting my hands free from their bondage. I reached out for him, but he took my hands between his, rubbing them to warm them up. He moved over me, pressing my hands back to the mattress. I could feel his cock right against my wet pussy. I tried to move him inside me, but again he evaded my every move.

'Fuck me. Please, fuck me, James. Fuck your beautiful wife right now.'

His smile disappeared and his hands released mine. I don't know where the condom came from, or how he got it on so quickly, but the next thing I felt was his cock, teasing me open. Slowly, so damned slowly, he slid inside me. I couldn't do anything but feel him, nothing else was getting through. All my senses were concentrated on his cock going into my cunt. I was babbling as he fucked me, my legs wrapping around his body. I was moving with him, letting him take me, my body offering up no resistance. I knew I wouldn't last very long; my body was so overloaded with sensation. With every slow, deliberate thrust, I could feel myself rushing closer and closer to orgasm. James grunted in my ear, his own pleasure evident. I felt full, stretched; my whole body felt like it was pushed to its limit. James swivelled his hips, grinding my clit against him before thrusting into me harder and deeper.

'Come for me, Sarah. I want you to come.'

Everything started breaking away, my mind falling to pieces as my body tightened under his weight. My pussy started to quake, pleasure bordering on pain shooting all through my body. I felt like I was being pulled apart by the joy of it all, his cock drawing every last ounce of feeling out of my body. I couldn't think or breathe. All I could do was come. It seemed like it would never stop, wave after wave crashing over me until I felt James drive into me harder, matching my climax with his own. It was so perfect, so sublime; I could hardly believe it was real.

Reality was slow to return. James rolled from my body and lay next to me, his strong arms refusing to let me go.

'So, my beautiful wife, did you learn your lesson?'

'I think so, but you never know. I might just need some more persuasion. After all, did you see my ass in those blue pants?'

A Lucky Man
by Lucy Felthouse

As a guy, I'm occasionally asked, 'Are you a leg, breast or bum man?' My usual reply is a smile and a shrug. Perhaps I'm then mistaken for a homosexual, because my response generally makes the poser of the question walk away in disgust.

It's not that I don't like women; far from it. It's just that I don't know the answer to that particular question. It shouldn't be such a difficult one, I know that. The problem is I like all three. So much so that I can't even begin to choose between them.

I like my women voluptuous. So to be asked to pick a favourite from an ample pair of breasts, spilling out from a corset, a fine ass in a figure-hugging pair of jeans or a sturdy pair of thighs capable of … well, use your imagination – it's just impossible.

I have a lady. I've actually just described her pretty well. She has the most magnificent pair of tits I've ever seen. I'm not a small chap and yet her breasts more than fill my hands as I knead, pinch and slap them. Likewise with her ass. It's firm yet pliable, and I love nothing more than to grab great handfuls of her bottom as we kiss, pulling her to me so our bodies mash together. Her thighs also drive me wild with desire. Those milky-white expanses of skin hold so much promise. They're capable of turning me into a pile of mush as she grips, tenses and bounces on me when we make love.

But I couldn't pick a favourite of the three. Her lovely legs, breasts and bum are part of her; they make her what she is. And I desire her more than anything. My sexy lady.

She *is* sexy, you know. She never believes me when I tell her, but she is. I look at her with her long, wavy chestnut hair, impish grin and startling green eyes, and I want her. Those stick-thin models and celebrities with jutting bones and concave tummies do nothing for me. Give me my beautiful shapely lady any day.

I love nothing more than to lay her down on our bed and worship her. I'll kiss her until we're both panting with lust, and then I'll start to remove her clothes. I start somewhere different each time, just so she doesn't know exactly what to expect. My favourite, though, is starting from her feet.

Say she's dressed casually: a jeans and T-shirt ensemble. I'll remove her socks, caressing her feet as they are revealed. I'll then slide a hand up each of her trouser legs, my fingers gliding along her smooth calf muscles. She always complains that they're too big and that she can't get long boots to fit, but I think it's nonsense. No skin and bone here, just beautifully smooth flesh and nicely tapered ankles, perfect for locking together around my back as we make love. I don't know what she's complaining about. Crazy woman.

Next I'll remove her jeans, flipping open her belt and button, then easing down her fly. I'll reach underneath her to grab the waistband, and she'll wriggle as I pull, revealing more and more of her tantalising flesh. Once the jeans are discarded, I'll lie flat on my front and bury my head between her thighs. My hands will be roaming, grasping at her buttocks and her thighs, pulling her fragrant pussy closer to my face. I'll inhale her scent through her scanty underwear, and groan appreciatively. My cock will already be rock hard.

I'll nuzzle at her now-damp crotch, teasing her sensitive flesh, a promise of what's to come. She'll start to moan, craving her release, but I'll unhook my hands from their fleshy playground and manoeuvre myself so I'm kneeling on the bed.

I'll hold out a hand for her to give me hers, and pull her into a sitting position. I'll whip her T-shirt off, sucking in an appreciative breath at the sight of her. A pastel-coloured stone will twinkle brightly from the middle of her gently rounded tummy, and her fantastic tits will threaten to pop out of her bra. They're traffic-stoppers, those. A danger to society. And what's even better, they're all mine.

By this point, I'll already be desperate to make love to her. There's just something so tempting about her. Her warmth, her softness, it all adds to my longing. I just want to plunge my cock into her, hear her moans in my ear and watch her beautiful face contort as she comes, pussy contracting around my cock.

But I'm getting ahead of myself. When I've managed to get a grip on myself after setting eyes on her heavily burdened bra and its contents, I'll slip a deft hand around her back and pop it open. Sliding the straps down her creamy shoulders, I'll plant kisses on each millimetre of exposed skin. Shoulders, arms, hands. Décolletage, breasts, nipples. Hips, waist, pubis. I'll slip my fingers into the sides of her pants and slip them down, my mouth heading southwards too.

She likes to style her pubic hair. Sometimes there's not a single hair there, and my tongue trails over naked flesh, delving lower until it slips between her nether lips and tastes her sweetness. Other times there is a landing strip, or a full but short bush. I'm not fussy. As long as I get to dip my tongue into her juices and make her writhe and gasp beneath me, I'm happy.

For the purposes of this particular tale, let's say that her pussy is completely bald. My tongue will practically trip over itself in its haste to pleasure her and hear those sexy noises she makes. The bare skin is even more sensitive and if I have stubble on my chin, she loves to feel it scraping against her, the abrasion inspiring a pleasure-pain reaction. She may gasp, but her pussy can't lie. It oozes juices, which smear across her ample thighs, and glistens, pink and inviting.

I will dip my tongue between her fleshy folds and taste her. Her natural lubricant is sweet, and the taste and smell simply act as an aid to turn me on more. My cock will definitely be making its presence known by this point, straining against the confines of my underwear and jeans. But it's not about me, it's about her. I am nothing if not a gentleman; I like to know my lady is satiated before I seek my own release.

My tongue will play in her pussy, smearing her juices all over her puffy flesh and swollen clitoris. I will lick and nibble and suck and tease, anything my lady desires. Should she arch her back in passion I will grab her ankles and push so her knees are bent up to her chest, exposing yet another erogenous zone.

Her tiny puckered hole resides between the finest buttocks I've ever seen. Smooth, pale globes of flesh, which silently scream at me to play with them. Grab them, squeeze them, slap them, part them … The latter is what I will opt for on this occasion, giving me easier access to her ass.

By now, it will be slick with the juices that have run down from her pussy. My tongue will delve deeply into the crevice between the ample mountains of flesh and seek the hidden treasure. Her simultaneous tensing and gasping will assure me that I'm in the right place. The tight ring of flesh will be trying to suck in my tongue as I probe and delve deeper, stimulating her sensitive nerve endings and causing her pussy to contract and expel yet more wetness.

One of my hands will slide up to her clitoris, gathering some lubrication on the way. I'll smother the swollen nub of flesh with her liquid arousal and then stroke it lightly at first, then will increase the speed and pressure as I continue to torment her ass. I will sense that her climax is imminent and replace my tongue with my fingers, sliding two straight up her now-relaxed hole, and my tongue will go to work on her clit.

She loves to have her ass played with. Whether during foreplay or penetration, it doesn't matter. She once confided to me that it speeds up her orgasm, and increases its intensity. That, my friend, is a valuable nugget of information that I have utilised again and again, for mutual benefit.

On this occasion, my fingers will be doing their work, thrusting in and out of her tight ass as I suck and lick on her pussy, teasing her to the brink of orgasm. I know, though, that I won't be able to keep her on the edge for long. I try to tease her and keep her teetering, but I know that soon my fascination will win out. I will grant her release and watch, transfixed, as her face transforms into one of agony and divine happiness rolled into one.

At the same time, I will be unearthing my cock from the confines of my clothing, ready to slide it deep inside my stunningly beautiful lady. It will be hot to the touch and oozing pre-cum. Both of these states will be increased further when I push into her tight velvet hole.

Seconds later I'll bury myself deep inside her. We will rock together, our bodies intertwined, her luscious flesh sliding against mine. Her erect nipples will scrape against my chest, providing extra stimulation for us both. We'll fuck in this way for a while, until I become frustrated at the limitations. From this position I cannot worship her in the way that she deserves. Her beauty is hidden beneath me. I will flip us over so she is astride me.

What I see when she is on top of me never fails to take my breath away; not to mention flood yet more blood into my shaft. Her luscious chestnut hair bounces around her shoulders, framing her face, which is all smiles. Her tits immediately catch the eye – how could they not? – hanging full and tempting like delicious fruits. I cannot resist a taste, licking, sucking and biting at them. She gasps and thrusts her jiggling flesh more forcibly into my face, inviting more, harder.

When I am done devouring her breasts, my hands reach around her hips to grab her ass – I can't help it. Her ass is full, yet firm, and it tenses and relaxes as she lifts and lowers her delectable cunt on to my cock. I'll squeeze and stroke her cheeks, maybe pull them apart and explore the tight little ring nestling between them. I daren't do it for long – if I trigger her orgasm, I'm done for. There's no way I can hold off when her velvet walls start to spasm and milk my cock for all it's worth.

Instead, I will move on to my last but not least love: her legs. All I can reach from this vantage point is her thighs. Planted either side of mine, she continues to rhythmically pump up and down and I feel her muscles tense and relax; the ample flesh is soft and oh-so-inviting. We are connected in the most intimate way and yet I want more, I always want more. I cannot get enough of my buxom babe.

Another reason I adore my lady's figure so is that it is strong. Feminine, and yet solid. I know that we can play rough and she can take it. She loves it as much as I do, if not more. I'll grab her hips and force myself up into her. My cock sandwiched between her engorged folds, her juices sliding out and smearing over my lower abdomen, her clit brushing against me.

We are on the verge of a frenzy. Once we cross the line, there's no going back. It's a race to the finish line, except we aim to cross it together. I'll reach between her legs and stroke her clit – it doesn't take much. Soon she is crying out and her pussy is driving me to my own climax, its tight squeezing and releasing causing me to spurt my own violent release.

I'll pull her down for a kiss as we ride out our orgasms, my hand tangling in her thick mane, our tongues deeply caressing one another's mouths. Her arms will come to rest on either side of my head, her tits squashing against my chest. Then I'll roll her gently off me onto the bed and position myself so my head rests on her shoulder, her arm around me. From here, I can continue to caress her; my fingertips drift across her breasts, her stomach, an aimless pattern that relaxes us both.

This is a blissful ending to a perfect session. We have both enjoyed each other's bodies, and now we are taking comfort from one another in a companionable silence. I reach over her with my free arm and crush her tightly to me, silently expressing my affection and love for everything that she is. My love, my rock, my passionate and beautiful woman.

And after all that exploration, I still can't decide. Leg, breast or bum? My lady has all three, and they're all mine. I'm a lucky man.

The Beautiful Move in Curves
by Elizabeth Black

The more Olivia Taylor read, the angrier she felt. *Who the hell was this clown?* She felt the heat rise in her face as her indignation grew. Since Kevin was the only person within fifty feet of her, she dealt him a blast of her wrath. Kevin didn't mind. He was used to Liv's spirited tirades. She leaned on Kevin a lot. He was her favourite 'friend with benefits'. He was her trusty sounding board, and today he would hear how she felt very sore about such a moronic article. *This is not the sort of thing I should be reading only a few hours before speaking on a panel about how fat women are sexy.*

Liv was taking a break from packing their gear for the science fiction and fantasy convention they were attending. She and Kevin were manning their sex toys and erotic books table. When she was not scheduled to speak on panels, Liv would work the table with him.

Liv poked one manicured finger at the computer screen. 'Can you fucking believe this crap? This idiot wrote an article trashing women he thinks are too fat by calling them "butterbodies".' As Liv continued to read the article, her blood pressure rose with each word. 'You've heard of "butterface", right? She has a hot bod, butterface is so homely she could stop a sundial? Well, this is the reverse. Her face is smoking hot, butterbody is dumpy. He put Salma Hayek on his list of "butterbodies". Are you fucking kidding me? What guy in his right mind would think that *Salma Hayek* looks like a slag? He says she has a beer gut? She just had a baby, moron!'

Kevin dropped an armload of jelly butt plugs and thrusting rabbit vibrators into a box. 'Stop getting all worked up. You'll give yourself a stroke, and you aren't even fifty yet. This idiot is not worth it. He probably hasn't had a date in years, lives in his mother's basement and writes on his blog while stuffing his face with bags of crisps.'

'I can't help it. You do make me feel better, though. But I can't possibly feel good about my weight if some cretin thinks that Salma Hayek is too fat.'

'You look beautiful. Really, Liv. You are gorgeous, and you know it. Stop feeling so insecure. Remember – you're speaking on a panel about sexiness in a few hours. Do I need to give you a confidence boost? You look like you live on more than a bowl of lettuce every day. You're healthy and you glow. You know that.'

'Yes, I do, but I feel so insecure when I see all the thin, toned bodies out there, and here I am, close to 200 pounds, and I am too scared to go out in public because I think I look like a carpet whale.'

'Will you stop it? A whale should look so good.' She felt Kevin's strong hands work the taut muscles in her shoulders. She melted at his touch. He knew just what spots to press to relax her when she was tense. He was right, though. She *was* sexy. It was just articles like this idiotic 'butterbody' one that poked her most insecure spots.

'My, you are a bundle of tension. Do I have to put you over my knee and spank you?'

'I'm afraid Jeremy is going to take one look at me and scream.'

'Why would he? He knows you aren't one of those stick-figure models.' His hands travelled down until they moulded her large, firm breasts, one after the other. He lifted them and held them together until she stared down a well of cleavage. His thumbs and forefingers pinched her nipples until they stood erect and purple. The ensuing jolt travelled from her nipples to her crotch. *I feel a little warm down there* ... 'For one thing, you have the most amazing breasts. Your ass is round and gorgeous. Remember you sent Jeremy a picture? He even told you he thinks you're gorgeous. I can see he's right.'

'It's just this stupid web page that has me upset. You never see web sites trashing how famous men look. When men age, they become "seasoned". When women age, they are "butterbodies".'

'I don't know ... have you seen Clint Eastwood lately? Besides, you never liked the pretty boys anyway. You like brainiacs. Smart is sexy, after all. When most women melt over Hugh Jackman, you get weak-kneed over Gil Grissom on *CSI*. Grissom is a big, cuddly teddy bear. You tell me that all the time.'

'He's smart and eccentric. A lethal combination in my book.'

He stood behind her and placed his large hands on her shoulders again. She felt the electric shock of his touch, anticipating his next move. *His mere touch drives me wild!* 'Is it time to play our little game? Let me say the brainiac words that turn you on ...'

She giggled as his hands massaged away the tension in her shoulders. What would Jeremy think when he finally got a good look at her? Would he look at her in disgust and turn away? *Of course not!* He told her he didn't care how much she weighed. She was the sexiest woman he ever met, and they hadn't even met in person yet. He loved the pictures she sent him. He wanted a woman with meat on her bones.

She met Jeremy online at an Internet fetish group. An accomplished scientist, he worked for the National Institute of Health as a biologist. As soon as Liv learned he was a scientist, she was hooked. She lusted after smart men, and scientists were at the top of her 'fuck me' list. Then, they discovered that they had erotic fiction and sensation play in common, and they quickly learned that they were both polyamorous. He was only 31 to Liv's 48. Kevin called Liv his 'Sexy Cougar', and she couldn't get enough of it. At 28, Kevin was quite a bit younger than Liv. *I collect younger men the way some women collect porcelain dolls. But my men are not for show. I give them a workout!*

Jeremy said he thought Liv was the sexiest woman he had seen in years. Plus her open attitude and blunt way of talking about sex turned him on even more.

Kevin liked her that way, too. More to love. And he was about to give her just what she needed, all with a few well-placed scientific terms from her favourite television show that turned her on every time they played this silly game.

'I know just what to say to drive you wild ...' He leaned over and whispered in her ear, his deep voice growing gruff with desire. 'Gas chromatograph ...'

She giggled as his tongue flicked her ear. 'Now you're being silly.'

'Alleles.'

As the fingers on his right hand pinched her nipple through her T-shirt, his left hand reached beneath the flimsy cotton and grasped her bare breast. Liv never wore a bra. She liked the loose feeling she had as her large breasts bounced against her shirt. They sagged a little with age, but they were as firm and as large as they had been when she was twenty years younger. He gave her breast a quick squeeze, and the powerful stimulating sensation travelled down through her stomach and slammed into her pussy. *God, I want him, and I want him now ...*

'Did you lock the front door? I don't want people walking in the store with us carrying on like this.'

'Yes, the door is locked.'

'But the blinds aren't pulled. People can see in!'

'Can they? Good! A little exhibitionism turns me on. Now how about some more sexy words?' His lips blew butterfly kisses down her neck. As his tongue licked her warm, sweaty skin, she shivered in ecstasy.

'Luminol. Oh, baby, let me turn you on. Petechial hemorrhaging.'

Kevin pulled her leggings and black briefs to her knees. She smelled the sweat and juices from her moist pussy as soon as it was exposed to the air. *My, but I love that heady smell. It's MY smell!* Kevin slipped his fingers into her waiting crevice.

'How about a fish sandwich before we go?'

Before she could answer, Kevin's face dived into her pussy. He pushed her leggings and briefs past her ankles until they sat in a pile on the floor.

'Jump up on the table. I want to eat you.'

Eagerly awaiting his talented tongue, she leaped upon the table and spread her legs. His strong hands held her legs apart, and his face nuzzled her pussy. Within seconds his tongue lapped at her erect clit, driving her to an erotic frenzy. His lips sucked against her clit, pulling at it, making her feel so very weak in the knees. His index and middle fingers slid into her wet pussy, probing and massaging her G-spot. *He didn't waste any time. My G-*

spot was just waiting for him. She arched her back, pressing her warm pussy against his face.

He ate her out some more, licking and sucking until she was so aroused her body went rigid. She pinched her hard nipples, hoping to make them even harder. So sensitive were they that each pinch vibrated from her boobs down to her warm pussy. She felt her heart pounding as blood rushed through her veins, warming her all over. Closing her eyes, she saw the shadows of blood rushing back and forth like waves. Each pulse throbbed in her pussy and her throat. His tongue alternated between licking around her clit and against her pussy lips, and then sucking hard on her clit. She was ready to burst. *I'm so close I will spurt fluid all over his face if he keeps this up.*

She ground her pussy against his face as her bum lifted off the table. Upon hearing snickering, she turned towards the windows. Two men stared at her from the open window, wide-eyed and fixated on her writhing body. *We have an audience.*

She smiled at them and lowered the leg that was closest to the window so that they would have a better look. Cupping her large breasts, she squeezed them and pinched her nipples while staring at the men with her best 'bedroom eyes' look. Kevin was none the wiser, since his face was buried deep in her pussy, driving her wild. One of the voyeurs licked his lips, and that was all it took. Liv's orgasm rose from deep inside her body, and it exploded against Kevin's face. She ground her pussy hard against his lips as his mouth sucked hard on her clit, his fingers working her G-spot. She felt the moisture from a puddle grow under her bum. She rode the waves of her orgasm for over a minute until it subsided.

The two men clapped, catching Kevin's attention. He looked towards the window, saw the two voyeurs and laughed. The two men waved, cheered a little more, and fled, likely from embarrassment at being caught, and arousal on their own parts.

'I didn't know we had a command performance. I take it that was good for you?'

'Yes, both your mouth and those two blokes watching us.'

'I knew you were a bit of an exhibitionist. Having them watch really turned you on, didn't it?'

She only smiled, stood up and tidied herself. Kevin grabbed the bottle of all-purpose cleaner and a paper towel and cleaned up the puddle on the table.

'Do you feel better now?'

'Yes, sir. Much better.'

'Are you going to let articles written by cretins get on your nerves any more, at least this weekend?'

'No, sir.'

'Good! Now if you start to feel insecure again, I'm afraid I'm going to have to spank you.'

'I'll supply the paddle.'

They packed the boxes into their cars and headed for the convention. After registering and setting up their table in the dealers' room, Liv checked in and went to her own room. She unpacked her luggage and moved her belongings into their proper places. Clothing in the dresser drawers. Shampoo and conditioner on the tub. Curlers and make-up on the bathroom sink. She never felt completely at home in a hotel until she had unpacked everything. Once she felt settled, she opened the bottle of cabernet she had brought and poured herself a glass. The tart red liquid felt good flowing down her throat. She felt her body relax, and she knew the good times were about to start.

How about dressing up? I want Jeremy to see me

looking my best. Liv curled her bum-length auburn hair and put on a little make-up. *Not too much. I don't want to look like a tramp.* She reached for the rose cotton ankle-length dress she had brought specifically for this occasion, and slipped into it. After brushing out her hair, she inspected her appearance in the mirror. *Hmmmm. I do clean up nice. Jeremy will love the way I look. Kevin will be floored. He rarely sees me all dolled up.* She called the front desk to see if Jeremy Kingston had checked in yet, but the hotel clerk told her he had not. Disappointed, she left her room to wander around the convention before stopping at her table to help Kevin set up.

Kevin did a double take when he saw her. 'Well, look at you. You're the sexiest woman in the room. Dress up more often, Liv. You look smashing.' He poked her in the ribs and grinned at her. 'Expecting company, by any chance?'

'I wanted Jeremy to see me looking my best.'

'You always look your best, but now you look good enough to eat.'

'You already ate. Maybe later.'

'Don't dare me. I'll take you up on it.'

The con was packed. Liv was delighted to see a wide variety of body types as she wandered around the tables in the dealers' room. Women with hair down to their bums meandered between the tables, while other women with spiked hair every colour of the rainbow mingled with the crowd. Such a wide variety of people, which was to be expected at a science fiction and fantasy convention. Some walked about in costume while others donned comfortable T-shirts and jeans. While some of the younger women were quite thin, Liv was happy to see heavier women dressed in 'Buffy' and 'Firefly' T-shirts picking up a double dildo here and a bottle of massage oil there. And they shopped with their lovers! *Ha! Let Mr Butterbody see these women with their lovers, and call them fat and homely women who can't get dates. Loser!* These heavier women and their partners (both male and female) bought sex toys and massage items even before Kevin and Liv had completely set up the table. *Good! It's going to be a successful weekend! We're making sales already, and we aren't even set up yet.*

A tall, young man approached their table as Liv picked up a 24-inch bright purple double dildo. Liv's pussy melted at the sight of him. *Oh my God, he's here! Stay calm and don't do anything stupid.* Standing at six feet tall, his lithe body swayed as he walked towards the table. Dressed in black, from a black frock coat to black jeans and a tight black T-shirt, his body screamed 'fetish lover'. Black hair hung in his face, but it did not cover his electric blue eyes that were slightly almond shaped. There was nary a blemish on his café-au-lait skin. Dimpled cheeks were capped by high cheekbones. He grinned at her, and Liv grinned back.

'You must be Liv and Kevin. I'm Jeremy. Liv, your picture doesn't do you justice. You're simply stunning.' His voice was deep and as smooth as warm honey. Very hypnotic. He stared at the double dildo Liv held in her hand. 'Is that for me? I thought you'd want to wait before we got into the kinky stuff.'

'Oh my God! I'm so sorry,' Liv dropped the double dildo onto the table as if it were a poisonous snake. She ran out from behind the table and hugged Jeremy. *He feels so firm and strong, and he's all mine!* She ran her hands down his back, just resisting grabbing his delicious bum to give it a hard squeeze. His arms wrapped around her back, and he hugged her so tightly she couldn't breathe. Seeing Jeremy in person at long last felt as if all her dreams had finally come true. She hugged and squeezed him to make him feel more real. Her entire body tingled with desire as she took in his heady scent. *He smells like cinnamon and cloves. I could eat him, he smells so good!*

'I take it you've checked in.' She knew what Jeremy wanted. The same thing she wanted.

'Yes, although the room is a bit of a mess. But it's presentable.'

'How do you feel about a little privacy?'

'It's what I've waited for all year.'

'You two go and enjoy yourselves,' Kevin said. 'I'll mind the table. I figured you two would want some private time, anyway.' He held up a pair of plush handcuffs, and a huge grin spread across his face. 'Need anything to take with you? Cuffs? Butt plugs? Flogger whip? A third partner?'

'Kevin, you're so bad.'

'I have all the gear I need,' Jeremy said. 'Although I'd have to ask Liv's permission if she'd like a third person to join us.'

'How about I enjoy you alone first, and then later Kevin joins us. How's that sound, Kevin?'

'I'm game. I don't want to leave the table alone anyway. Too many tempting goodies here that hot little hands will swipe when we aren't looking.'

'Good point.'

'How about after the dealers' room closes for the night? Is that OK with you, Jeremy?'

So Liv was going to have hot monkey sex with both Kevin *and* Jeremy before the night was over. How exciting was that?

Liv's heart raced as she invited Jeremy into her room. While boxes were scattered about the floor, the room was tidy enough to please Liv. She took his black frock coat and hung it up.

Facing Jeremy, she took in his gorgeous body. Broad shoulders dressed in black silk tempted her. She wanted to rest her head on his shoulder while her hands roamed his strong chest. Although he was young, he looked a bit older than his 31 years. The long hair that hung in his eyes and brushed his collar gave him a nonchalant air, but his bright blue eyes looked alert, as if they didn't miss a thing. His gaze was deep and penetrating, and at that moment his gaze was firmly fixed on her face. The unspoken question was obvious, and Liv knew what to do next.

'May I hug you?' she asked.

'Yes. I'd like that.'

Oh, to finally touch him, to caress his body. Her arms shook as they wrapped around his back. The scent of cinnamon and cloves floated in a cloud around her head as she rested her head on his shoulder. Heart racing, she pressed her body against his, feeling his slender form mould into her own. While Jeremy wasn't muscular, he was slim and strong. Just the kind of man she loved the most. All those years teaching judo had paid off. His body felt deceptively slight, but she knew he was strong enough to throw a grown man across the room.

She raised her head, and their lips met. His tongue slid into her mouth, and she tasted coffee and chocolate. The luscious taste combined with the smell of cinnamon and cloves made her head spin.

They wasted no time. Liv had waited for this moment for a year, and she didn't want to wait any longer. His firm hands found her breasts and squeezed, sending pulsations of pleasure from each breast to her pussy. Her pulse quickened, and she felt the blood rush into her pussy. *I'm horny again. I want this man in my bed, and I want him there now.*

After a frenzy of removing their clothing, they were on the bed, tearing at each other, devouring, kissing, sucking and petting. *I can't keep my hands off of him! I want him so badly!* His hands found the flesh around her belly and squeezed it, moulded it, until his erect cock pressed against her thigh. His breath felt hot against her skin as his mouth pressed against her throat, trailing down until his lips wrapped around her hard and sensitive nipples. Each nibble at her buds sent shock waves to her hot and wet pussy.

'My God, your body is so beautiful,' his voice was deep and raspy with desire. 'I think about you every night before I go to bed, and I've imagined this moment for many months. I feel as if we are already lovers. You know what I want now, don't you?'

She turned over on to her stomach, and his hands found her full bum. He squeezed each bum cheek, and then without warning, one hand came down on her with a resounding *smack!*

The sting felt sharp and glorious as painful sensations rammed into her pussy. She spread her legs to give him greater access. Two fingers slipped into her pussy as yet another finger found its way into her anus. She smelled strawberries as he opened a bottle of lube she had placed on the dressing table, and within seconds his hard cock made its way into her ass. Spreading her legs to accommodate him, she took in every inch of his erection, and his fingers found her clit, massaging and pinching until her body shivered with arousal. He grew even larger as he slammed into her, his fingers pressed against her swollen clit, and his other hand coming down hard on her bum cheek with a loud *smack!* With each spanking her pussy tightened until she finally exploded with the most amazing orgasm. As she rode the waves of her climax, Jeremy burst into her ass. She felt his cock jump with each pulsation of his orgasm. Jizz trickled down her cheeks.

Spent, they both turned over on their backs, chests heaving with exhaustion. After a year of flirtatious and erotic e-mails, they finally consummated their relationship.

'That was as wonderful as I had dreamt it would be. Liv, you are absolutely beautiful and the sexiest woman I have ever met.'

'You've been my dream lover for as long, too. I'm sure we'll continue where we left off later today.'

Her dream finally came true. Jeremy's body was all she had hoped for, and more. Liv knew that she and Jeremy would hook up again several times before the convention ended. She saved the under-the-bed restraints, ball gag and spanking paddle for the evening. She hadn't had a threesome in several years, and Kevin would be game to join them before the weekend was out. That idiot who wrote the 'butterbodies' article didn't know what he was talking about. She knew she was sexy – sexier than those stick figure women who were so thin their ribs showed. And she had the sexy, younger men to prove it. Liv vowed never to read such articles ever again. They weren't worth her time or attention.

Chocolate Lover
by Victoria Blisse

She moaned and threw back her head in delight, her thick thighs rubbing together of their own accord as a bolt of sensual pleasure coursed through her body.

"You like that, don't you?" her husband whispered, stroking the side of her large breast with a teasing finger. "Do you want more?"

"Yes," she said, her dark eyes shining.

"What's the magic word?" he teased, leaning closer to her, pressing into her curves.

"Please?" she begged, eyes wide, lips pouting.

He nodded and slipped another square of milk chocolate between her lips.

"Chocolate lover," he taunted, and she winked at him as she sucked the chocolate into her mouth and felt the creamy comfort of it melting over her tongue.

"Now that would be something I could sink my teeth into," she purred then licked her lips.

"I remember that time with the chocolate body paint," he said, "I ended up covered in bites and bruises."

"I don't remember you complaining at the time." She reached out to him and stroked his erection through his trousers. "Do we have any of that left?"

"Hmm, I don't think so, but I have a sweet treat here for you."

"I can tell," she purred and pulled open his pants. "I hope it has a creamy centre. That's my favourite part."

"Oh, it's mine too." He licked his lips and watched his sweet-loving wife lavishing affection on his cock.

She treated it like an expensive bar of chocolate. Delicately she licked, relishing its flavour and texture on her tongue. Teasing herself to a point when she needed more she engulfed the thick head with her lips and sucked the solid bar, enjoying the warm hardness against her tongue and relishing the gasps and moans she pulled from the lips of her lover.

"Fuck, I'm going to melt in your mouth," he groaned and thrust his hips, forcing more of his cock between her enticing lips. He wrapped her dark locks around his fingers in an attempt to control the pleasure exploding through him but the tightening grip in her hair made her suck harder, heightening the erotic tension in his dick.

She could still taste chocolate on her palate and, mixed with the salty sweetness of the juices leaking from his tip, it proved to be a seductive concoction. She could not get enough of it. Up and down, slowly and steadily she sucked, mimicking the dance of sex, feeling the phantom memory of his cock in her cunt. She could tell that he was close to coming: his balls were tightening beneath her fingers and he was panting and thrusting up into her mouth with increasing urgency.

She loved this moment the most, the moment when he cursed and screamed and roared as he surrendered to the pleasure and the cum erupted into her eagerly sucking mouth. She savoured every last drop then grinned broadly.

"I do love that cream filling," she said.

"Is it tasty?" he asked, basking in the joy of release.

"Sure, taste for yourself." Before he could protest, her

lips were on his and they were kissing. He was surprised to find he didn't find the taste repulsive; in fact, it was an arousing reminder of the blow job he'd just received, and the sweet lingering hint of chocolate on his wife's lips gave him a wicked idea.

"Happy birthday, darling!" He rolled over to her side of the bed and wrapped his arm around her soft waist.

"Thanks, sweetheart," she pushed her plush arse back into him, feeling his solid cock between her ample buttocks. "What have you got for me this year?"

"Oh, I have something very special for you," he purred and kissed the sensitive spot at the base of her ear. She moaned and reached to cup his cock.

"Oh yes, it feels very special," she gasped. He pulled her hand away from him and moved it back over her waist.

"No, my love, that isn't the present I was talking about, although I do plan to give you *that* as a bonus if you're a good girl."

"I am always a good girl," she giggled and shimmied against him, which caused his arm to rub against her breast as her buttocks shuddered against his hard-on.

"Oh, baby, I know," he groaned and cupped her tits through the thin cotton of her nightdress, "so very, very good."

"So what have you got for me?" she whispered. "I'm curious now."

"All in good time, my love, all in good time." He pressed her back into the bed and flipped over her leg to rest between her thighs. "I want to play with my good girl for a bit first, now you've got me in the mood."

"You're always in the mood." She shook her head, smiling seductively. "It's why I married you."

She lifted her bum as he rolled the material of her

nightie higher and higher, revealing her thighs, her rounded stomach and the tips of her tightened nipples. He continued to pull the material up and over her head, until it came away completely and he threw it down to the floor.

He pulled her arms back above her head and captured her wrists, holding her in that position as he plundered her mouth for a kiss. His lips trailed lower, and his fingers tickled down her arms, landing on her ample bosom. He squeezed and moulded its heavy heat as he suckled, and then his mouth travelled lower still, his fingers staying to feast on the abundance of her breasts.

The tip of his tongue teased the gentle dip of her belly button. She giggled and squirmed at this intimate and subtle touch. He continued to kiss over her stomach, tracing the silvery lines that caressed her sides like fine lace and treasuring every soft, giving inch of her.

"Please," she whimpered, her skin on fire with desire, her mind blinded with lust.

She felt his smile against the under curve of her stomach. He made every inch of her feel sexy, even the parts that she was uncomfortable with. His lips pursed and kissed and moved lower, and she forgot all her self-centred worries and fears as passion wiped everything else from her mind.

He was trying to tease her, but the closer he got to his goal the stronger her scent was and the weaker his resistance became. His pace quickened, and his kisses stopped lingering and gained purpose as he trailed through the curls over her pubis. His tongue slipped down and traced the path between her parted sex-lips. He probed deeper and her juices coated his tongue and filled his mouth with mellow sweetness.

She gasped as his tongue moved higher again and his

lips fastened around her aching clit. She moaned and pushed up her hips as he sucked rhythmically, teasing pleasure from that central point and sending it coursing through her entire body.

She was close to exploding: her skin was feeling tight and almost painful, her brow was prickled with sweat, her cunt was so wet she could feel her juices flowing over her thighs and between her buttocks. She was seconds away from coming all over her husband's face when he stopped.

"Bastard!" she cursed, and he just laughed.

"Now it's time for your present." He stretched out, opened the drawer in the bedside cabinet and withdrew a cylindrical wrapped object. He passed it over to his wife who pulled herself up into a sitting position and ripped open the bright, star-scattered paper.

"It's your cock," she gasped, cradling the phallus in her hands. "It is, it's exactly the same." She lifted the heavy object to her lips and gently slipped it between them. She sucked briefly then groaned, "Chocolate, I love chocolate."

"It's a chocolate lover." He grinned, grabbed her legs and pulled her back down the bed. She screamed and then groaned as he plunged his cock into her without any preparation.

"Suck it, suck that cock while I fuck you," he begged and she pulled the chocolate back to her mouth and plunged the creamy hardness inside. She yelped but the perfect replica of her husband's cock in her mouth muted the sound. She felt so dirty, filled at both ends by two big, heavy cocks. She was caught between her two loves, chocolate and him. She was in heaven.

"Fuck, you give good head," he groaned as he watched her intently, admiring her sweet mouth at work. He thrust forward, feeling her cunt spasm and suck around him, and the combination was more than he could take. Aware of his gaze resting upon her lips she slipped the sweet cock deep inside her mouth and, as he watched, she swallowed it down to its root. The lewdness of this act pushed him over the edge. He roared and filled her with his cum.

"I need to fuck you with that cock," he gasped as he pulled out of her. He took the replica dick from her hands and teased the sticky head around her cunt lips. He could see his cream inside her and, as he pushed that chocolate cock in, his juices oozed out around it. He couldn't help himself. He had to taste that heady mix of her musk, his salt and the mellow sweetness of her chocolate lover. He tasted it all as he slipped his tongue around the cock buried in his wife's pussy.

She writhed on the bed, her chocolate lover slowly melting inside of her. It felt so kinky to have her husband's mouth licking and sucking around the cock buried within her. He pulled and pushed the dick forcefully and fucked her thoroughly with it, lapping up the chocolate and cum displaced by the violent fucking.

"I'm going to come," she gasped, and he moaned, pulled back and watched as her fingers snaked down to her clit and began to rub over it roughly.

"That's it, baby, come all over your lover's cock. Yes, cover that cock with your juices while I watch. Fuck yes, that's it."

She exploded at his words, screamed and felt the chocolate give and ooze as her cunt spasmed and her orgasm forced itself free of her body. She moaned as the cock was drawn from inside of her, but the moans turned from disappointment to lust as she saw her husband eagerly sucking her juices off the chocolate phallus.

"Suck that cock, baby," she gasped, "suck it clean."

He looked at her, his bright eyes wide with desire, his lips stretched lewdly around the chocolate. He pulled the dick from his mouth and offered it to her. She eagerly took it and plunged it into her mouth. She could taste her sweetness mingled with the creaminess of the chocolate as it melted into her mouth and dripped all over her lips.

Their gazes never drifted from each other, and she watched her husband lick the chocolate cum from all over his lips. A jolt of desire shocked through her body and vibrated in her freshly fucked cunt.

When his gaze finally left hers it travelled down her curves and her still splayed thighs. With a sexy eyebrow shrug he dipped his head and she anticipated the caress of his lips on her sex. She sucked eagerly on the pleasure-giving chocolate in her mouth as his lips and tongue hesitantly swept over her chocolate and cum-covered cunt.

He was overwhelmed by the scent. The chocolate was heavy and cream laden, his cum was a more astringent scent like lemon juice and he could pick out the peachy freshness of his wife's juices that pulled the two opposing scents together and blended them like a top chef creating a new recipe.

It was appetising, and he wanted to taste it, but it was something so new, so different that he hesitated a moment, and just looked at her creamy, chocolate-filled cunt. It was beautiful, like a skilfully crafted dessert. He almost didn't want to ruin it, he wanted to look and watch and treasure this moment without taking the next step.

It was her moans and her hip thrusting that fuelled his desire and encouraged him to take his first taste of chocolate cream pie direct from her hot, wet hole. It was the chocolate he tasted first and so he dug a little deeper and found the scent and taste of his wife. It made his cock jump. It was the next thrust that revealed the salty undertone of his own cum to his taste buds, and he found himself licking and sucking in earnest, wanting to taste more of this lustful creation.

It was sex, pure and simple in a taste. It was kink, it was love, it was arousal, it was them and it was all in a taste that bathed his tongue. It was almost too much to take, but it was so addictive that he wanted more, and with each mewl and gasp from his wife the desire to taste more became stronger.

He licked her hole clean and moved on to her lips and her clit and chased the last traces of this unique taste sensation across her intimate parts.

"I want to taste you now," she groaned, and he scrabbled to move around on the bed. She rolled to her side and cradled his head on her thigh as he continued to lick with barely a pause. She passed the chocolate cock to him and pulled him closer, her hand squeezing his tight buttock as the tip of his cock slipped between her lips. She experienced the same taste as her husband, the chocolate was already in her mouth with hints of her and him, but the warmth of his turgid flesh transformed it from just taste to pure desire.

They were joined together by a taste, by a bond, by a moment of sheer desire and new discovery. They were both burning with need and their mouths worked in rhythm with each other to bring ecstasy to their partner. She groaned and gasped and took more of his hardness into her mouth as she felt the chocolate cock pressing against her tight rosebud. Her anus eagerly opened to accept it. She felt her husband's cock expand in her mouth as her chocolate lover slipped into her back passage.

His lips locked on to her clit as the chocolate moved in

and out of her tight hole. It felt so dirty, so naughty to be fucked back there as her husband ate her cunt. It was like a decadent orgy and she was the centre star with two dedicated lovers using her plush body for their own pleasure.

She loved being that slut, that receptacle for lust. She rocked her hips in time with the cock in her arse, and she ground her cunt onto her husband's face as she came hard with a scream that was muted by the cock in her mouth. Moments later she felt and tasted the flood of her husband's desire and the drip of the chocolate oozing from the shrinking cock lodged in her bottom.

"I love you," she gasped, swallowing his cum and licking her lips.

"I love you too," he groaned as he pulled away from between her thighs, pulling what was left of her chocolate lover with him.

"Thank you for the threesome," she smiled as they untangled and rearranged themselves head to head. He kissed her and they shared the lingering flavour of lust once more. "That is now officially my favourite way to enjoy chocolate," she said.

"I agree," he replied. He had become a chocolate lover too.

Mama Nana
by Alcamia

One day, I met Mama Nana and I fell in love.

At the time, I was living with my sister Simone in Paris, and she suggested I pay a visit to a small local haunt, called the Tidy Bar. 'There's no place like it, Michael, you'll absolutely love it,' she enthused. 'It's a shabby-looking place on the outside, but it's owned by the fabulous Nana, and the ambiance and jazz piano are out of this world.'

The Tidy Bar was innocuous; it had dirty windows and a faded sign, and from out of the door, which was always open, trickled the delicious aroma of exotic food and the clink of frequently refilled glasses. It was enough to make me salivate and so, I was soon to find out, was Nana.

I decided to take my current girlfriend, the svelte and fabulous Maxine, to the Tidy Bar. Maxine possessed a lithe, athletic body. She had long, elegant limbs, which she stretched and flexed constantly, and musculature that would not have been out of place on a racehorse.

'Shit, there's a birthday party going on,' Maxine whispered behind her hand, as she sat down with a sigh at the table. 'I think we ought to leave. I hate loud birthday parties, don't you, Michael?'

'No, we'll stay. Despite appearances to the contrary, I have it on good authority that the food here is to die for.'

Shrugging, Maxine arrogantly flicked her long hair out of her face.

I heard Nana before I actually saw her. As I was soon to discover, everything about the astonishing Nana was larger than life, and her voice was as astounding as the rest of her. It had the musical quality of a husky jazz singer, low and mellow, with a mellifluous seductive undertone, punctuated with raucous and highly infectious laughter. It was a sex voice, so alluring and dirty you couldn't help turning to see where it was coming from.

Maxine leant across the table. 'Good Lord. Did you ever hear anything so loud, and did you see the size of her? It's indecent. It shouldn't be allowed in public.'

Mama Nana presided over a table like a queen holding court, entrancing a party of men. I swear I'd never seen a woman quite like her before. She was striking and so overblown that she made me blink. Nana's skin was the colour of ebony, and she had a pert mouth and white teeth that flashed joyously when she laughed. Her hair was braided in a complicated confection of corn rows and ersatz paper flowers and she wore a bright jungle-patterned corset which forced her breasts up like two meringues over the fabric.

I stared at her and Nana looked up, winked at me and, opening her mouth, saucily pushed in a whole caramel éclair and licked the cream from around her lips with her pink tongue. I dropped my knife with a clatter, and my cock, which until this moment had been dormant, leapt to attention. I was fascinated by Nana because I'd rarely seen such fulsome beauty. My cheeks burned bright red. It was instant attraction, instantaneous mental and emotional bondage.

I can divide my life into two distinct time periods: pre-Nana and post-Nana. When I was in pre-Nana mode I would never look at a woman more than a size twelve. I was attracted to slinky, feline women with attitude, and the slimmer the better. I adored staring at girls in low-slung hipster jeans, with flat bellies and non-existent busts exhibited beneath knitted skin-tight tank tops and T-shirts. I admired their fragility and flat bellies. I got off on the thought of running my hands over perky little tits and flat, sexless bottoms. I think I enjoyed boyish nubile fragility and observing the frantic way my lively dick burrowed away in small, tight holes. I mistakenly thought my psychological profile dictated that to experience an earth-shattering climax, I needed the lithe sinuosity of athletic shapes and emaciated bodies to feed my fantasy.

Maxine sprung to her feet, overturning her chair with a clatter. 'You can't take your eyes off her, Michael. Whatever's wrong with you? Why do you keep staring at that oversized whore? I'm leaving.'

'Fine by me,' I said with uncharacteristic levity.

To be honest, I felt as if my eyes were cemented to Nana by some form of sexual adhesive. This was the time before cigarettes were banned from cafés, and I watched, hypnotised, as Nana took tobacco out of a beaded pouch and folded a roll up with her bejewelled fingers. On the table was an ivory box and out of the box she extracted a long amber cigarette holder. The men rushed forward like wasps circling a honey pot, clamouring over delicious Nana. Young boys, older men, nobody seemed immune to her larger-than-life, femme-fatale chemistry. They all leant forward flicking lighters and striking matches, while, roaring with laughter, Nana waved her hands, finally accepting a light off a pale blond boy with hair down past his shoulders. Her wanton decadence amused me.

I'm a writer and I like to think I'm a good observer of

human behaviour, but I'd never observed behaviour quite like Nana's. Already, I was in a state of rampant and agonising arousal, and I don't think I'd ever experienced such a hard-on. My dick was instantly so rigid it was pressing painfully against my zipper. In a desperate attempt at relieving myself, I had to make a rather unsatisfactory exit to the gents' toilets, where, slamming the door, I set to work liberating the bony reprobate and giving myself a most satisfactory hand job to the distant musical accompaniment of Nana's mirth.

Mama Nana reminded me of a girl called Benita, whom I'd met when I travelled to New Orleans. It struck me now – as I suffered another bolt of agonising arousal – that Nana shared the strange sexual aura as Benita. Benita had been a huge woman by anybody's standards. She'd seen me staring and fixed me with her black eyes. Splaying her huge legs, she flirted with me while sucking me down into a deep tingling pool of excitement. Her skin glistened and she had a manner of stroking her long fingers very suggestively through her sleek black hair. I'd had the best affair of my life with Benita, who seemed to experience joy and orgasmic overdrive in any position or place I cared to name. She would wantonly strip off items of clothing and display herself whenever she felt like it. I experienced torrid sex in doorways and streets and up against lampposts, and with this sex came a liberation I'd never had before. Benita's voluptuous body encompassed me and squeezed the sex out of me like a sponge, and I loved every moment. Voluptuous sirens, I discovered, seemed to possess a magical property which the slimmer girls did not, namely a feral abandonment, and a certain joie de vivre coupled with the most insane sexual appetite. I'd do anything to date a slim woman but my libido never responded in quite the same way as it did to a damsel of extravagant proportions. It was as if my dick assumed a whole new identity with the Nanas of this world and it couldn't wait to escape my pants.

The Tidy Bar didn't close very early, and the door remained open. It was a sultry and oppressive night. A waiter brought out a brimming meringue confection and the flock of assiduous studs sang "Happy Birthday" while Mama Nana, pursing her large and luscious lips, blew out her candles with a giggle.

As the night wore on, I watched, mesmerised, as Nana became sexually looser, her laughter more basso profundo and suggestive. Each time one of the men caused her to giggle, it was as if he depressed a magical switch and Nana's Rubenesque physique trembled with volcanic intensity. The delight rose up from her belly and her frame trembled with erotic promise, each inch of her delectable flesh rippling like molten lava. The pale boy sat on her lap and, as she stroked his hair, I saw his hand slip down between the folds of Nana's corset to caress the jiggling breasts. The scene reminded me of the way my grandmother fondled her cat; but there was a great deal of affection in the purring fondling, and there were sexual undercurrents in the air that crackled like electricity. Cutting a slice of cake, Nana fed it to the blond youth, who licked the confection from around his mouth while Nana dabbed at his lips with a napkin. A large breast had somehow struggled free of her corset and I felt my heart palpitate as her huge, black nipple perkily angled towards me in greeting. Soon I noticed the hand of one of the men sliding up Nana's thigh, higher and then higher still. I'm sure that hand stayed under her skirt for quite some time while her lover manipulated her fanny, because a strange erotic brilliance lit Nana's eyes, and she seemed thoughtful, as if she were holding her breath. The thought of the hand and what it was feeling really fired me up. I was uncomfortably hot and aroused, stirred by salacious sexual sensations and awakenings.

Gradually the men ebbed away and the bar emptied. I realised there was nobody left except me and Nana, who every so often dipped her finger in the remains of her cake and, holding it up and looking at me, inserted it suggestively into her mouth. 'Come here, sexy,' she said, crooking her finger and sitting down at the piano. 'Come and join me. You look lonely without your girlfriend.'

Her fingers rippled up and down the keys, and Nana began a low resonant humming. She was an incredibly good pianist and she had a seductive blues voice, which could have put many professionals to shame.

'You have a great voice.'

Nana winked at me, flashing her incredible teeth. 'Yes, I have many talents, or so I'm told.'

I could have listened to her all night, but eventually Nana stood up and went and sat back down at the table. 'You look very sad without your girlfriend.'

'Oh, not really. Maxine wasn't my thing. She had an extremely short fuse.'

'Thin women always have short fuses,' Nana said. 'That's because they spend too much time analysing and stopping what goes into their mouths and it makes them irritable and sexually dry. I live for sex, you know, I'm a sexual machine, there's nothing better than a fabulous shag. Personally I never worry about what goes into my mouth or the fact that I'm just a little on the large side. I indulge myself and the food gives me pleasure. It stokes up my sexual machinery. I simply love food and wine and men.' She leant closer to me. 'My darling, I adore fucking and plenty of it with lots of variation. The happier I am and the more I eat, the more elated I become, and the more mind-blowing the sex becomes. You know, I've had many lovers, and they all find me adorable.'

I was so intrigued by Nana I believed I was within the firm bondage of a witch of the pleasure variety, and she'd woven a spell of cosmic enchantment over me.

'You have a naughty look about you with those cunning devilish eyes. I love a man who puts his soul and all of his feelings into his eyes. I can also tell you're dying to stick your dick inside Nana.' Saucily cupping her breasts in both hands, she did a shimmy, and for a flicker of a second I had a fabulous view of her other extravagant breast.

I noticed she wore coloured sandals with beads, and each of her toenails was painted a different colour. I was sure I'd never seen feet quite as beautiful as Nana's; they were small and perfect and they were so smooth they looked like a child's. I had a sudden urge to sink on to my knees and take Nana's feet and caress them. I wanted them in my hands, in my mouth, tickling my cock.

'You're so sexy and you have a really cheeky little cock,' she whispered huskily, her hands combing through my hair. 'How do you fancy a real woman, because I could certainly eat you all up?' Then she gave me a wry smile.

My eyes dropped lower to her heaving bosom, and I was delighted to see that the other breast that had been threatening to escape from Nana's excruciatingly tight corset had now succeeded, and its warm, textured, satin nipple was tentatively brushing my arm. My hand, seemingly assuming a life of its own, was compelled to reach out and touch the tantalising flesh. I trailed my finger down her cleavage and Nana shrieked with enjoyment. The shrieking seemed to once again set in motion her body, which began to surge and tremble like some wonderful fairground ride. Her breasts shuddered and shook and her nipples, if it were at all possible, hardened even more invitingly.

'I want to fuck you, Nana. I want to fuck you in every possible way I can think of.'

'Oh! I know that.' Before I could stop her, Nana's hand was on my crotch and she had fastened her long fingernails around my cock. Grinning at me, she began to squeeze harder and harder until my alarm changed to pleasure and the pain became an erotic charge. My dick jerked and jumped as Nana gripped it with even more ferocity. 'It feels so lively, I expect it would enjoy being buried up to the hilt in Nana's mountain, wouldn't it?' She sighed as her arm snaked around my waist while her other hand began to dance up and down my pole, long fingers stroking and scratching, rubbing and squeezing. 'Ooh, you're such a big, juicy boy.'

I wanted to pillow my head on her huge breasts, be consumed by the bounteous corpulent generosity of both her body and spirit, lose myself in the deep velvet prison of her sex. With a suffocating sense of joy my whole being tingled at the thought of becoming lost in a copious ocean of rippling, sexually potent flesh. 'Oh, you're gorgeous,' I said.

Nana's bedroom could not properly be called a bedroom at all; boudoir would have been a better word for it. It was as if she'd infected the room with her decorative and flamboyant nature. The ambiance was one of simmering sexual anticipation, an unctuous confection of scents and colours and opulent decadence. I threw myself down on the ornate Spanish bed and spread out my limbs on plush, thick cushions while Nana treated me to a fabulous striptease. First, she unlaced her corset, teasing me with the sight of her quivering huge breasts and fabulous tits. Then, placing her leg on the bed, she slowly rolled down her stockings. Unfastening the catch of her skirt, she let it fall away to reveal her curvaceous hips. Licking her lips with her little pink tongue, Nana began to roll and knead her sumptuous flesh before kneeling on the bed and lowering herself perilously close to my rearing organ.

'Would you like Nana's big bazookas on your little friend?' Nana crooned as she massaged the impressive breasts with her hands. 'Well, oil them for me, darling, and in return I'll treat you to such a surprise you won't believe. You see, I do so love having my tits and cunt well oiled.' And, winking at me, she handed me a pot of sweet-smelling oils. Nana took my hand, pressed it to her huge bosoms and made me fondle and caress them until they shone like two pendulous black pearls. Nana leant right over me and, encompassing my cock with her breasts, she pressed together the huge cushions. Effectively sandwiching my now bursting cock, she made me slide up and down her cleavage until I exploded. Nana gave a wild whoop of delight, kissed me hard on the mouth, reared up and slathered my copious ejaculate on her tits before leaning back, pushing her finger under her knicker elastic and coyly pulling the panties aside, vibrating her voluptuous hips. I couldn't take my eyes off the sexy black panties that held the luscious, ripe, wet fruit beneath them because Nana was wet, very wet. She eased down the tiny slither of silk to reveal her plump, cavernous sex with its inviting, pouting lips. I swear she had a sex big enough to match her girth; it was amazing, a generous tasty feast waiting to be assaulted by my aching cock.

'Come and see what Mama Nana's got for you,' she crooned, holding open her arms and wriggling her tongue suggestively. I pushed my face against her engorged, soft breasts, tugging at her tits and sucking them. After a while Nana let out a cry of orgasmic excitement, so I slithered down her body and set to work on her cunt, burying my face between the trembling thighs and thrusting inside the warm world of Nana. I was an explorer setting out on a vast continent of promise. I can tell you, a size zero never presented such a plenteous panorama of possibility. When my cock eventually sunk in her lubricious, wet folds, Nana held me and rocked me. I now metamorphosed into a ship afloat a wide, tempestuous ocean. Floating smoothly along, I was subjected to a licentious feast of calm sailing, punctuated by a maelstrom of passion that threatened to throw me loose from my sexual life raft. The huge breasts moved beneath my hands like two liquid-filled life buoys and, as if my life depended on it, I clung to them. The harder I clung the more Nana rocked and rolled.

'I think you much prefer Mama Nana to your tiny friend, don't you? Now you've had champagne mama, you'll never settle for cheap vin rouge?' Nana broke once more into gutsy laughter while, wrapping her huge legs around me, she gripped me in a suffocating bear hug. That was the icing on the cake, I can tell you, as the erotic sense of suffocation only heightened my ardour.

There's no other woman in my life now because Nana understands all my quirks, and I will never tire of plotting my charted course across her vast and intriguing continent. Actually, I don't think there's another woman in the world like Mama Nana.

Two for One
by Kitti Bernetti

Craig's eyes popped wide awake as one hand clamped sharply over his mouth and another invaded the space between his thighs. Before he knew it, a blindfold had been forced over his eyes and now was firmly fixed so he couldn't see a damned thing. His heart thumped. What the hell was this?

'Don't move … Yet.' The woman's voice was young and breathy with excitement. Craig lay motionless on the pillow, his world an inky blackness. 'Sod it,' he thought. If only he hadn't drunk quite so much last night he'd have woken up before this assault. Usually he slept lightly. But not when he'd had three courses for dinner, and two bottles of vintage champagne. The hotel room was quiet, the air conditioning gently humming. The only other sound was the low, sultry laugh of the woman next to him. What crazy sort of game was this? He listened for clues. He'd have taken bets she wasn't skinny. That laugh was too rich, too full of honey, too resonant to come from anywhere but an ample chest. Craig wasn't a small guy. Tall, with a strong jaw and long legs, he was what you'd call rangy. Some might say skinny. Suddenly, something stirred deep within him. Fright mingled with desire. He'd never been trapped by a woman before. It was usually him doing the entrapment. Knowing he was the powerless one sent his imagination running wild.

The vague scent of Chanel perfume eased its way from the girl's wrist just below his nose into his nostrils. He breathed deeply, nervously trying to guess if it was No. 5 or No. 19. Not sweet enough for No. 5. Definitely No. 19. Nice. But scary. Was this a joke or some sort of robbery? If she was after money, she was in the right place. Craig had been doing all the buying for his team last night. Aperitifs, liqueurs, the lot. He'd had a wallet full of cash and only spent half of it. But then, if she wanted to rob him why hadn't she just done it and gone. No. This was about something else entirely. The girl's long hair tickled his face as she leaned closer. He guessed he was right about one thing. He reckoned she was a big girl. He could swear he felt mountainous breasts overflow on to his arm. God, he wished he could see them. Warm, soft, powerful. Her skin brushed against his. Her voice penetrated the darkness. 'Listen. Don't budge. I'm going to remove my hand in a minute and we're going to trust you not to yell.'

We?

'And do you know why we can trust you?' Craig took a risk and shook his head slightly. 'Because if you don't do as you're told, my friend has her hand ready to cup your balls and squeeze. Hard.' Craig nodded as he registered the pressure of not one but two female bodies under the sheet beside him.

That voice? He tried to make out which of his sales team it could possibly be. They'd all drunk far too much after last night's awards ceremony and true, he'd flirted with them all in turn. He must have gone a bit too far. And now they were getting their revenge. They didn't call his team 'Craig's harem' for nothing. But the girls knew it wasn't serious, didn't they? He flirted with all women, all the time. That's why he was so good at his job. Sex sells, ask any ad man, and although Craig promised, he never delivered. He didn't believe in mixing business with pleasure. If he was a woman, he'd be called a prick tease. Funny there wasn't an equivalent name for a man who liked to promise but didn't deliver.

Craig had been doing it for years. It got him just what he wanted. Usually. Top sales figures, awards. A pay rise after schmoozing the girl from Human Resources. Now, it seemed someone wanted what they felt was due to them. Slowly the hand was taken off his mouth and he whispered, 'What do you want?' The blood rushed in his ears so loudly he almost didn't hear himself and was about to ask again when he felt the hand on his thigh start stroking. Craig held his breath as the hand moved upwards. She didn't grip his balls, she just started kneading them gently. Teasing. Craig held his breath until the need to breathe, to pant got the better of him.

'I said don't move,' came that rich, commanding voice in his ear again as he felt her slide down and start twirling her tongue around his nipple. 'We need you rock hard.' The other girl had started running her nails sharply up his thighs. Expertly, she pulled in her claws as she teased soft fingers around the base of his penis. Craig tried to get his brain into gear. It wasn't easy. Most guys would think they were in seventh heaven but Craig was pissed off. He didn't want his body to react like this, he wanted to be annoyed and shout at them for breaking in to his room. It was a damned stupid prank. But with the sort of attention he was getting he could feel himself hardening by the second.

With his last ounce of reasoned thought, his mind went back to whom he had lent his room key to earlier. Sarah. That must be who it was. His forehead frowned under the blindfold. Quiet, mousy Sarah whom he had to send on assertiveness training? Surely not her. But, yeah, he had lent her the key so she could come and fetch the brochures for their display. Was she a fulsome girl, well covered like these two? It was impossible to tell with those nondescript dresses she wore. Now his prick was not only being held but was being expertly massaged up and down by girl number two. She'd used some sort of lube, something delicious and creamy slipping and slurping up and down him. Her hands, her fingers, were working overtime on Craig's straining shaft. She was getting him ready for something. The air was dense with anticipation. He could hear her now, as she edged down the crisp white sheets to kneel in front of him on the bed, her knees either side of his. Her touch was gloriously unbearable.

But, those keys, he fought to concentrate. Sarah may have borrowed them but it was Louise who had given them back. It couldn't be feisty red-haired Louise though. She was the one member of his team who'd never looked at him twice. She had the truest hourglass figure he'd ever seen. A gloriously huge rump as round as a racehorse and monumental freckled breasts that spilled out against half-buttoned business shirts. All the guys in accounts talked about was sinking their faces between those two superb mounds of womanhood. But Louise wasn't having any of it. With an athletic fiancé on the go she'd been immune to Craig's go-to-bed eyes.

The girl at Craig's knees now cupped him in both hands, and he was no longer frightened of her firm grip. She obviously had only one thing on her mind as he felt her moist lips close over his tip, lapping it like an ice cream cone. Craig moaned, and then he heard her say, 'That's it gorgeous, get going, get nice and horny 'cos it's nearly time for you to do some of the work.' That voice. It could have been Miranda; she was a dark horse with those sultry, deep brown eyes. But no. She had an accent. It wasn't her. While he was trying to think clearly, he was aware of the girl lowering her fantastic round breasts over his hard cock. She was squeezing them together, tormenting him, pushing her breasts up and over his cock rhythmically. He felt his mutinous penis give in, loving it, wanting it more and more.

A second later, Craig was aware of girl number one straddling his face as she held on to the headboard. Beautiful, generously proportioned thighs trapped him in their hot grip. 'OK,' she ordered, 'I'm ready for you now. I'm sure your tongue can do more than just sweet-talk women.'

Craig obediently opened his mouth and she lowered herself on to him, exuding the bittersweet womanly musk of a girl close to coming. He worked not only his tongue but his fingers over her swollen clit. Sucking, licking, teasing, lapping, he couldn't get enough of her. She was like an over-sweet ripe peach as he drank her in. She was delicious, practically suffocating him, then lifting herself to give him air before descending back to cream into his waiting mouth. Moving his hands up to clamp her thighs, he moved her sex down, in and out of his mouth, tonguing her like a cat greedily finishing a bowl of cream. As he rocked his head back and forth, he felt her hand come down and grip his hair, pushing him deeper and deeper into her as she suddenly cried out into the night air, tumbling into a crashing orgasm, then pushing herself heavily off him and landing sated and spent on the sheet next to him.

All the while, the other girl had been working away at his rock-hard cock, and now he heard her speak. 'It's my turn now. Get on top of me,' she ordered. Oh my God, it must be Rosalind, thought Craig as the girl lay down underneath him, and he grasped one stupendous breast in his hand, directing it towards his mouth. Rosalind with the long, blonde, straightened hair. He moved his hand up to grasp her hair and find her out. At the same moment he drove his massive steel-hard erection inside her. She was soaking wet. She also wasn't Rosalind, he realised as his hand cupped the back of her head and discovered short, thick, lustrous hair.

By this time he had stopped wondering. What the hell did it matter? The blindfold could stay on if that's how they wanted it. He needed a long, hard fuck so bad, and by the sound of her so did she. Up and down rammed his hips as she raised hers higher, higher. Then he reached down, found her ankles and hoisted her legs either side of his shoulders, opening her wide to him. She was superb, massive, every bit of her was in gorgeous widescreen technicolour surround sound. 'Right there, right there,' she cried out, 'don't stop, don't you dare stop.' He'd obviously hit the spot, pounding deeper and deeper into her as she bucked and writhed. The headboard thumped over and over until he shot his load into her, sweating as she shuddered, rose and came underneath him.

Craig had often been told off for falling into a deep sleep the minute he'd come. By the time he woke up they'd both gone. It could almost have been a dream, apart from the state of the bed and the unmistakable, perfumed musky Chanel smell still embedded in the sheets.

In the morning Craig showered, packed, put on his suit and a clean shirt, not bothering with his tie, and went down to reception to check out. There stood Rosalind and Sarah and Louise and Miranda. His eyes flicked from one to the other of them. Which two girls shared that amazing secret? Which two had given him the best night of his life? They all looked tired. 'Sleep all right, girls?' he asked boldly standing near them to catch a whiff of that Chanel 19. There it was, unmistakably. But it wasn't coming from them. It was coming from behind him. He whirled his head to see the two girls at the reception desk whom he had flirted with when they had greeted him yesterday and who had access to all the room keys. One a long-haired beauty with a breathy voice, her voluptuous, larger-than-life curves forced into a sensible business suit. The other a tall, no-nonsense German girl with short, thick hair, an Amazonian bosom and a wry smile.

'Hope you enjoyed your stay, sir,' she said, raising her perfectly plucked eyebrows, 'do come again.'

Workout
by Beverly Langland

I think I am about to die. I sweat while those around me glow. For the past forty-five minutes I have managed to keep pace with the rigorous aerobic workout, but now I am ready to drop. If hell is worse than this I'd be surprised. Still, I carry on – as I always do – driven by the dream that one day I too will be in as perfect condition as the young, pretty instructress Sandi. I know my expectations are unrealistic. I have put myself through this self-induced torture for over six months and haven't lost any weight of significance. It is time to face the truth. I will always remain on the plump side no matter how hard I work, how much I wish otherwise. The health club subscription has been a waste of money. I'd have been better off buying some magic knickers.

By the time Sandi finally calls a halt to the carnage I feel so exhausted that I vow never again. There was a time when a woman's curves were appreciated. Sadly times have changed. It isn't as if I'm unhappy with my body. Until recently I had been more than comfortable with the way I look. It was only when I met Roger that I started to have doubts. Not that Roger says anything directly, but the odd derogatory comment has crept into his conversation. Little things that undermined my self-confidence and with everything on the high street geared towards the ridiculously emaciated, I decided to give aerobics a try. Hence the torture. The pain. All for a man. Good God, what on earth am I doing, trying to buy into an image I don't believe in? Well enough is enough! If Roger doesn't like the way I look, then tough. There are other things about me other than my body which are pretty wonderful.

Standing under the shower, I let my mind float away in the misty warmth. Soon, the hot burning needles start to soothe my aching muscles, but as the pain fades so does my resolve. Roger is a good catch – handsome in a rugged sort of way and fairly successful at his job. I know Roger has his faults but it isn't as if suitable replacements have been queuing to usurp him. I could do far worse. With soap in one hand and a soft terry cloth in the other, I scrub away at my underlying feeling of discontent. I summon an image of Roger in my mind and try to invoke a sense of belief. As the shampoo suds drain from my body, I softly caress my soapy breasts; dutifully wash between my legs – perhaps paying a little more attention than strictly necessary. I have no idea why I feel starved of affection, yet I am elated when I touch myself. I quickly check I am alone. Hot steam fills the white-tiled room, obscuring my errant hand, hiding my hideous body.

To ease my sense of guilt, I imagine Roger slipping into the shower with me. I take his cock in my hand, guiding the head between my bloated lips. He slips easily into me from behind, burying his hardness deep inside as I lean against the wall, the water spraying in between us, on my back, on his front. Roger thrusting, me accepting, my breasts swaying as he thrusts hard, taking me deep and fast. Roger always takes me from behind – without fail. I appreciate this makes it easy for him to think of someone else. I try not to be upset by his transgression. It is not a crime for him to imagine I am someone beautiful, but once – just once – I wish I could look into his eyes to see if the love he professes is real.

A sound breaks my reverie. Startled, I open my eyes to be confronted with the beautiful smile of my blonde instructress. Sandi has removed her headband; her long straight hair hangs delicately over her shoulders and breasts. A pink nipple peaks impertinently through the wet strands. From this distance her youthful face looks more like that of a twelve-year-old. I explore her lovely, shapely body with envious eyes – marvel at how perfect she seems to me, how exactly she is what I desire to be. For a moment I find myself blatantly gaping at Sandi's naked body. Her small up-turned breasts resemble those of a young teenager, though her best physical feature is, without a doubt, her firm, round bottom. I have been transfixed by those firm buttocks on many occasions. Yet, what draws my attention is Sandi's smoothly shaved pubis. I don't know why this should be; after all, shaving is hardly uncommon. Still, my eye is drawn to her sex as the young woman soaps herself without inhibition, running a finger deftly between youthful pouting lips. Her eyes are closed under the spray of water, but I'm certain I don't imagine the wry smile. I tear my eyes away when I realise my fingers are still moving – only to notice another woman has been observing my interest in Sandi. She watches me as intently as I had watched the young instructress.

The woman's presence takes me completely unawares. I have seen her in the gym before, yet we have never spoken. The woman is incredibly muscular, and obviously works out in the weight room. Her body looks magnificent, almost Amazonian in physique. She is almost the opposite in every respect to the petite Sandi, yet in her own way is uniquely beautiful. Naked in the shower with these two women I become incredibly self-conscious of my size, of my lack of dedication. My body is no temple. Shame-faced I turn away. I want to rinse off quickly and get dressed, want to hide within layers of baggy material, to run away from prying eyes.

"Need someone to wash your back?" Before I can think of anything to say, I sense someone close behind, then feel the unmistakable nudge of erect nipples against my back. I freeze beneath the hot water. "It's Julia, isn't it? There's no need to hide from me." Strong hands circle my waist; turn me slowly until I reluctantly face the dark-haired Amazon. I am immediately struck by the intensity of the woman's eyes – as wide and as blue as a clear Mediterranean sky. I can see my own startled face shrinking away in the reflection. The woman has washed away her make-up and her short wet hair lays plastered against her head. Her features are striking – she is more beautiful, more youthful than I first thought. The Amazon's voice remains low, almost husky as she whispers close to my ear, "I just love big tits." She reaches out to caress my left breast. Stunned by her boldness, I look around in alarm. Sandi has departed. There is no one to help me. "Don't worry, there's only us two …"

"That's hardly the point!"

"You prefer your girls boyish, like that waif Sandi?"

The young woman had obviously formed the wrong impression. She thought me a lesbian, but even if I were so inclined I'm not the sort of woman who is into public displays. I live a safe, boring life, munching chocolate with one hand, while with the other I switch channels with the TV remote – searching for answers. "It's not that…"

"What then?"

"I hardly know you …" I realise how feeble my protest sounds, especially as the muscular brunette already has one of my nipples between her lips. I stifle a moan as the young woman draws the hard pebble deeper into her hot mouth then proceeds to nip excitedly. The hot water coupled with the girl's ministrations has a profound effect on me. I should never have touched myself! I am already aroused and when she takes hold of my hand and places it on the back of her head; I draw the girl to me. The Amazon lets out a muffled moan and snakes her hand along my thigh. At first, as foreign fingers draw close to my sex I recoil, then finding myself pressed against the cubical wall I put up token resistance while the woman's fingers persist. They search my hairy muff. I can't remember being so wet, so excited. I wrap my hand in the young woman's hair and lift her head onto my other nipple. She moans and sucks on it greedily.

Suddenly, she pulls away. Her eyes are shining, full of mischief. "Here, let me." Her strong hands are already caressing my shoulders, my arms. Reaching past me, she grasps the hanging tube of soap and begins to lather her own body, concentrating on her breasts, her tummy, her pubis, her thighs. I watch transfixed as the water runs in rivulets through her soft pubic hair to cascade off her pussy. Covered in lather, she smiles slyly, replaces the soap and turns me to face the wall. I feel her lean against me, feel the firmness of her youthful body against mine, feel her soapy breasts rub against my back. Her hands reach around to cup my breasts with her soap-filled hands, squeezing them, cleansing them, tweaking the nipples until they are erect and impossibly hard. I feel so stunned I don't resist as she manhandles me. I do nothing – say nothing – as her insistent hands venture to my tummy, briefly lower …

Quickly turning me around, she continues to rub her soapy body against mine, driving me almost mad with passion. Not knowing what to do, I raise my hands and put them on top of her head, working lather into her scalp. She lets me know she likes this, immediately fondling my soapy breasts, lightly pinching and squeezing my hardened nipples in response. She takes the bottle of gel, squeezes a blob onto her palm, then cups my pussy and works the lather into my hair with the heel of her hand. The Amazon takes her time, stroking me gently through my curly bush with her fingertips. It doesn't take long for her expert fingers to locate my burning clitoris. One touch and I know I am too far gone to resist whatever she intends next or to even care who walks in and catches us. I close my eyes as the Amazon's fingers work their magic, occasionally they dart from my throbbing bud to delve into the depths of my quivering vagina. After a time, she takes one of my hands in hers and guides it between her legs.

We remain so engaged for some time, standing face to face, each gently soaping the other, neither saying a word. I continue to wash until the girl moans and starts to hump against my soapy hand. The Amazon, slightly taller looks into my eyes. I can only imagine what she is thinking, can only guess why she is attracted to me of all people. Yet she obviously is. My own mind is a ball of confusion. Why am I doing this? Besides the obvious pleasure I feel in having the young woman's fingers coax my clitoris into the open? She smiles as if reading my thoughts, steps closer and draws me into her strong arms. Once again I feel her soft, soapy skin slide over mine, feel her breasts flatten against my heavier chest, feel her firm abdomen against my belly, feel the tickle of her wet thatch of pubic hair as she squeezes against my thigh. The Amazon starts to move, making small gyrations to ensure the transfer of suds from one body to the other. She rocks gently from side to side, pressing tit-to-tit, rocks back and forth against my thigh. I join her, mimicking her sensual movements.

As the warm water cascades over us she covers my mouth with hers, holding my head in her hands. She tastes of mint. Her tongue thrusts into my mouth and I suck on it hungrily. Instinctively, my hands find the perfect globes of her bottom and I pull her tight against me, lifting her onto my thigh. After a few minutes sliding her wet, soap-slippery body against mine, her fingers spread my bottom cheeks and she pushes a digit against my rear hole. The sudden incursion has me squirming away. The Amazon puts more soap on her hands, rubs my crotch in a long arc from the top of my pubic hair back between my legs to the cleft between my buttocks. She deliberately presses her finger a little harder each time she skirts my anus. I feel more comfortable with her probing now. I know I am clean. She touches the hole gently with the tip of her finger and I feel my muscles clench. Yet, the soap makes her finger so slippery that when I relax the tip of the digit enters – just a fraction of an inch. She keeps her finger in the centre of me and wriggles, her other hand gently soaping my pussy, fingers sliding between the swollen folds. Amazingly, I begin to push back against the invading finger, encouraging, forcing a little more inside. The finger slips inside to the first knuckle. I tense again and squeeze, but the Amazon resists the pressure. Her finger remains lodged, edges deeper. I enjoy the sensation, turned on by her resolve, by her forcefulness.

She slips a thumb inside my pussy. I moan contentedly, begin to move my hips in a slow, circular motion. The woman responds, wriggling both her thumb and the finger in my bottom. Just when I think it is too much she somehow manages to rub my clit. I feel inner muscles tighten around the thumb; feel my sphincter clench so tightly I am afraid I will snap off her finger. I begin to tremble, recognising the signs. She recognises it too. Suddenly, the young woman pulls the finger out of my arse. The sudden loss sends me over the edge. I come violently, clamping my thighs together and trapping the girl's soapy hand with her thumb still buried deep inside me.

The Amazon isn't satisfied and after a few minutes of continuous worming, nor am I. Her undiluted enthusiasm drives my arousal to a new high and as another orgasm nears I cry out in encouragement. In response, the young woman slips two fingers inside my pussy and sets to work in earnest. I brace one hand on the cold tiles of the shower as she holds my hip and pumps into me. I am taken by surprise with the ferocity of the woman's frigging. It verges on viciousness and at times I feel as if the strength of the girl's fingers literally lifts me off the floor. I feel powerless to resist and something about the woman's unbridled strength fuels my excitement. As the frigging gains pace my orgasm builds until I feel my legs wobble. I have to hold on to stop myself from falling.

"Oh, God," I moan softly, the sound barely audible above the spray of water and the echo of slapping fingers. Now, her frigging is almost brutal. Her fingers move with me, move against me. I drive my hips backward as she pushes forward, urging her to fuck me – harder, faster, deeper. My heavy breasts swing fiercely, slapping together with each powerful thrust. "Oh my God!" I repeat, my entire body shaking as orgasm sweeps through me. This time my legs buckle, but the Amazon holds on tight, keeping me upright as she pounds into me a little longer for her own gratification. When I eventually open my eyes her face is inches from my own. The eyes are intense, yet they are smiling. I can find no malice there.

I pull the Amazon to me, shoving her against the cold shower wall, and press my exhausted body to hers. She gasps in surprise as her flushed skin touches the cold tiles, but I quickly place my mouth over hers, stifling any protest. Now, *I* am searching, probing. I want to give in return but have little idea what she wants. My fingers find her softness and I insert two soapy fingers into her. The woman begins to breathe harder as my fingers set to work. I am hungry now. I want to devour her. Like something possessed I finger her, all the while keeping her pinned against the shower wall with the weight of my body. I feel her shake as she approaches orgasm, wiggling and squirming against me as if trying to escape. I won't let her. In a moment of inspiration I remove my fingers, take the showerhead off the wall and aim the spray directly towards her crotch. The Amazon gasps and opens her eyes wide as the hard jets of water catch her full on her most sensitive spot. She raises herself up on to her toes to meet the onslaught. Her eyes meet mine as the sensation overwhelms her. I soak up her look of adoration. For the first time in my life, I feel I am doing the fucking and not simply getting fucked. I like the feeling. I like it a lot. Even after she is spent I am reluctant to let the feeling go.

The Amazon's name is Helen. I decline her offer for a night of wanton debauchery. I'm not sure I'm ready for a lesbian lifestyle. As exciting as the encounter was, I crave cock too much. To change now would be a bit of a culture shock. I don't hate men, I just hate the way they treat me sometimes. Helen smiles ruefully. I recognise the smile for what it truly is. She too is used to disappointment. I think of Roger who will be waiting for me, scales in hand, of *his* look of disappointment. This stunning young woman on the other hand had not judged me and it felt so good to be held like a person and not an object. Helen had also given me a bloody good workout. I think I'd expended more calories in the last hour than I had in the last six months. I am tempted to change my mind and go with her. I know I should be wracked with feelings of guilt for even considering Helen's outrageous proposition. Surprisingly, I'm not.

Painted Lady
by Amelia Fox

WANTED: Rubenesque woman to life model for artist, two hours a week.

Virginia rang the doorbell and waited, still amazed at herself for answering the advert. She'd nearly chickened out twice, but her new resolution of seizing life's opportunities when they came had held fast and now she was standing on the doorstep of a man she'd never met, her dressing gown in a carrier bag, about to take her clothes off.

The man who opened the door didn't conform to any of her preconceived ideas of a painter. He was tall for a start – easily six feet – and broad shouldered. This man certainly hadn't been starving himself in a garret for his art.

"Virginia?" he asked, holding out his hand for her to shake. "I'm Patrick. Please come in. I hope you don't mind stairs."

She shook her head and followed him up what seemed like endless flights until he ushered her into his studio at the top of the house.

"If you'd like to get undressed over there" – he pointed to an antique silk screen placed across a corner of the room – "and then come out in your dressing gown when you're ready."

She pulled off her T-shirt and jeans, draping them over the top of the screen, and then hesitated a moment before adding her underwear on top of them. This man was going to see her naked, what did it matter if he saw her knickers as well? Though, as she belted her dressing gown around her, she wished fervently that she'd splashed out on something a bit sexier than her tatty old towelling robe.

She padded back round the screen, the floorboards warm under her bare feet, and the smile Patrick gave her made a tiny pulse start jumping between her legs.

"I'm going to start with a couple of quick sketches until we find a pose you're comfortable in and then we'll get to work on the painting." He nodded to a chaise longue in the centre of the studio. "Start by lying on your front, arms folded, head resting on them and turned towards me."

Taking a deep breath, Virginia let her dressing gown drop to the floor and did as he said. She watched him as his eyes flicked from her to his sketch pad and back again, connecting briefly with her gaze. Charcoal whispered over paper. Virginia's nipples tightened as she felt his stare travel over her back, her buttocks, her legs.

"God, you have a really amazing bottom," he said.

She blushed.

"I meant to draw! To draw!" he said, turning as vermilion as one of his paint tubes. "But I like it on a personal level as well," he added.

Before Virginia could think of an answer, he became businesslike again. "OK, could you turn over for me, please? Arms above your head, any way they're comfortable, right leg straight, left leg bent a little at the knee."

She rolled on to her back and, as her breasts moved

from their warm nest on the chaise longue into the studio's air, her already aroused nipples stiffened into two dark pink peaks. She heard him swallow.

"Let me know if you're too cold," he said.

She met his eyes and gave him her slowest, most sensual smile. "I'm fine."

He shifted a little on his stool, turned over a page in his sketchbook and began to draw her again. By the awkward way he was holding the pad, she could tell he was trying to conceal his erection, and she felt the first trickles of wetness start to flow inside her.

After five minutes he sighed and put down his stick of charcoal. "Something about the arms isn't working," he said. "Try putting one by your side. No, that's not it either."

"How about this?" Virginia suggested. She shifted up the chaise longue to let her head loll back over the rest, cupped one of her heavy full breasts so that the nipple peeked out between her fingers and let the other hand rest between her barely parted thighs.

"Yes," he said, clearing his throat. "Yes, that's perfect."

As he started to draw again, she closed her eyes, slipped her forefinger between her labia and began to circle it on her clit with the tiniest of movements. Her moist flesh felt like wet silk and her clit throbbed and swelled under her fingertip. She closed the fingers of her other hand, teasing her nipple, and felt a spark shoot down her body to her groin.

She heard his sketching falter, then stop. Opening her eyes, she saw he'd put the sketchbook aside and was watching her, making no attempt now to hide the bulge in his trousers.

She let her legs fall open, showing herself to him, and

dipped her first two fingers inside herself before returning them to her clit. Lifting her head, she looked at him. "Come here," she said.

He didn't need asking twice. Kneeling beside her, he took her other breast in his hand and drew her nipple into his mouth, first running his tongue around it and then sucking it until she groaned with pleasure.

He kissed his way from her nipple down the swell of her breast, pausing to nuzzle for a moment in the centre of her cleavage. Virginia moved her hand out of his way, and he ascended the other breast, circling it with tiny kisses before covering it with his mouth as she cradled his head.

He was stroking her now, his fingers slowly brushing over the deep curve from her waist to her hip, then onwards, down the outside of her thigh, across her leg and back up the inside, towards her still-rubbing fingers.

"God, you're wet," he breathed, as he touched her. "You're the most sensual woman I've ever met."

Gently taking both her wrists, he returned her hands to cover her breasts and then moved to the foot of the chaise longue and parted her legs further. Starting just above her knees, he pressed a kiss to the inside of each thigh, slowly working his way up until she felt his lips brush over her clitoris, and a shudder rippled through her whole body. One more touch, she thought, and she'd be coming harder than she'd ever come in her life.

He stopped and Virginia almost screamed in frustration.

"I want to paint you," he said.

"What, now?" She couldn't believe it.

"Yes. Trust me."

She watched as he quickly shed his clothes then picked up a palette and loaded it with paint. Rummaging in a jar crammed with brushes, he picked one out and dipped it into a jug of water before coming back to the chaise longue.

Virginia was transfixed by the sight of his cock bobbing towards her. It wasn't much longer than the average six inches, but its girth was impressive. She imagined how it would feel stretching her open as it nudged inside her, and her hands strayed downwards again.

"Wait," Patrick said. He was standing over her now, palette balanced in one hand, brush in the other. Before Virginia could ask him what he was doing, he touched the brush to her skin and painted a long curl of vivid blue, starting at her collarbone, swirling around her breast, over her stomach and coming to rest with a delicate flourish at the top of her bikini line.

"There's no finer canvas than a woman's body," he said, washing the brush and then mixing a brilliant green on the palette.

Virginia lay there and let his brush stroke her, a thousand times more delicate than his fingers had been. The trails of cold paint brought her skin up in goosebumps.

"There," he said, stepping back to admire his work. "Come and take a look."

Taking her hand, he helped her up and led her over to the floor-length mirror in one corner of the studio.

Virginia gasped. The swirling pattern he'd painted over her skin enhanced her figure, her hourglass shape glorified by its wrapping of painted ribbons.

"See how beautiful you are?" he asked.

Virginia nodded.

He turned her round and kissed her, softly at first, then growing into something harder, greedier. Without lifting his mouth from hers, he pulled her back to the chaise longue and sat on it, positioning her astride his lap.

Virginia felt his cock rubbing against the soft folds of her stomach and moved forwards and up, pressing against the hard shaft to open her labia and bring her clit into contact with it. She began to move her hips: up, down, towards him, away from him, using his cock to pleasure herself.

He tipped his head back and groaned as she coated his cock with her juices. Virginia could feel the heat growing inside her, her clit pulsing as she ground it against his hot, hard flesh. Raising herself up, she inched forwards once more so the tip of his cock slid into the opening of her cunt.

He groaned again and tried to thrust upwards, but she knelt up so that just the first quarter inch of him stayed inside her. "No, Patrick," she chided. "It's your turn to lie still now."

He stared at her and for a moment Virginia thought he was going to simply plunge into her, but after a few seconds he nodded and let his hands fall to her thighs.

Virginia lowered herself a fraction further on to his cock and began to slowly move her hips, gently pulling his cock from one side to the other as she gyrated. She could feel her cunt stretching wide to accommodate him, running with wetness to ease his passage into her.

She lowered herself on to him a millimetre at a time, a thrill spasming through her with every new nerve ending his cock touched, until finally she'd taken his full length and sat astride him, triumphant, his cock buried to the hilt inside her.

Her cunt muscles flexed involuntarily and Patrick's hands tightened on her thighs. "You can move now," she said.

He slid his hands up to her buttocks and cupped them, using his hands to indicate the rhythm he wanted her to move in. She picked up his tempo and slid up and down his shaft, searching for the angle she knew would bring her clit into contact with his body. She leaned backwards, arching her spine, thrusting her breasts forward. There!

"Oh fuck, that's good," she gasped, as her clit rubbed against him and his cock squeezed her G-spot with every stroke. The dry paint on her body was making her super-aware of every movement she made; it pulled at her skin as it moved, like a million tiny fingers.

Patrick reached up to her breast, stroking the hard nipple with his thumb, while his mouth fastened over her other nipple, sucking, teasing, licking and sending jolts of sensation down her body to collide with the ones his cock was causing below.

She could feel her orgasm building and rocked against him faster, riding him harder, wanting every last bit of that deliciously thick cock to be buried deep inside her as she came. She clamped her cunt muscles tightly around him, working towards the explosion she knew was imminent. He was thrusting now too, deep, deeper, deeper still, until finally, with one sharp cry, she went over the edge, the spasms radiating out from her cunt and through her body.

She felt his cock start to pulse in response, swelling even more thickly inside her, and then he was gasping her name, pumping into her, as she shook with the last tremors of her orgasm.

Sticky with sweat, paint and cum, Virginia lifted herself off him and collapsed beside him on the chaise longue. Patrick reached out and carefully brushed a strand of hair from her eyes.

"I think you're going to be a terrific life model," he said. "Can you make the same time next week?"

The Ivory Tower
by Izzy French

Charlie nudged the heavy oak door shut with her hips, and walked slowly towards her desk, her stockings making a satisfying swishing noise. She couldn't believe she was here at last, finally ensconced in her very own ivory tower. That they'd let her set up office at the top of the folly in the corner of the university quad. There were all kinds of ghostly legends attached to it, that's what had deterred anyone else from claiming it as their own, but Charlie wasn't the superstitious kind. The beamed circular room with leaded windows did appeal to the romantic in her, of course, but the best thing about it was that, finally, she was alone. Just her and her laptop. And wireless Internet access, of course. All mod cons, obviously.

Now she could get on with the task in hand. There would be few interruptions. She'd had a phone installed, but she doubted it would ring often. No, most of her communication would be via email. And that suited her just fine. She wasn't sorry to leave the huge open-plan university admin office behind. Most of her colleagues were girly and giggly, surprised when the phone rang, or emails pinged into inboxes, expecting them to carry out some mundane task. Charlie wasn't naturally arrogant, but she knew she was good at her job, that she buckled down and got on with it. Which was why her request for her own office, though it had raised a few eyebrows, had been respected. Finally she could escape the constant teasing, which she took well, she thought, despite its personal nature.

"Lock up your chocolate biscuits, Charlie's on the prowl," was one she heard often. She'd like to have said the old ones were the best, but they weren't. And if she'd been the sensitive type she might have thought the teasing bordered on bullying. But years of listening to it had toughened her up. And, anyway, if she wanted to she could lose weight, start a diet. Tomorrow. Be skinny like them. But, deep down, she loved her curves – they were hers and hers alone. Where would she be without them?

She twirled around in her new chair, taking in her new surroundings, fantasizing about being someone other than Charlie, university administrator, in charge of timetabling courses as disparate as comparative religion and particle physics. Today, if she wished, she could be Rapunzel. She let her head fall back and shook out her hair. OK, like most heroines Rapunzel was blonde, probably a size 8, and wore flowing velvet robes. Whereas she was brunette and a good size 18, but at least her hair was long and curly. And her outfit was somewhat more modern, dating from the 1940's. Her plum suit was sharp and fitted, leaving little to the imagination. Charlie loved the vintage look, though it wasn't always easy to find in larger sizes. Women had been altogether more scaled down back then. But the one she wore today clung to her curves like a glove. And she was a firm believer that if you felt good you looked good too. Not that there was anyone around to confirm or deny this; but, just for her own satisfaction, Charlie flipped open her mirror and re-applied a slick of deep red matte lipstick, gave her plump round cheeks a smile, and wiped a tiny smudge of eyeliner from the corner of her eye. She'd do. From the outside Charlie looked quite the part – smart and slick, though, just for her own satisfaction, her suit was covering, well, very little. Down below, at least. She couldn't go bra-less; that would be altogether too indecent. But she was a big fan of stockings and suspenders. And today she'd chosen to go without knickers. Just the thought made her want to rub her thighs together, send shivers of pleasure through her cunt, use her hand to treat herself to just one tiny little orgasm. She began to rub her thigh, tuck her finger under the hem of her skirt; but then she pulled herself together, placed her hands on her keyboard. There was work to get on with.

. She got up from her chair and turned the key in the lock. No giggling girlies or doddering dons would be pestering her up here today. She tapped away for an hour or so, cutting, pasting, and emailing attachments to stuffy old professors who were almost entirely unaware of how to open them. But that was their problem. There were only a few who regarded communication as a two-way thing. And some of them chose to moan and complain, flying into the old office, arms flapping, corduroy jacket flying behind them, demanding that she didn't schedule them for a lecture in post-modernism on a Friday afternoon, as it clashed with an important PhD tutorial. Charlie would smile and nod, knowing full well that the tutorial was in fact a date with a bottle of single malt, and move the lecture one hour later, once the infuriated professor had made his point and left the room. There was the odd one or two with whom she'd built up good virtual working relationships. Flirty, even. Professor Markham, and Dr Neilson, amongst others. Though she'd often wondered what they'd think of her if they ever met. Whether they'd be surprised or disappointed that she didn't resemble her peers, or live up to their fantasy of the ideal secretary. And she wondered too, if she'd be disappointed in them. Whether she'd sigh and let her shoulders drop when she noticed the patched jacket elbows, the bleary eyes looking over half-moon glasses. But then why should they conform to stereotypes any more than she did? That was why flirting by email was so much safer. There was so much less to lose.

Charlie tweaked a complicated spreadsheet for a while, then decided she deserved a little light refreshment. She flipped on her kettle, and began to prepare hot chocolate. She enjoyed her drink without the raised eyebrows, and the 'what does she expect if she drinks that' glances crossing the room. Taking her first, and most satisfying, sip she jumped at a sharp rap on the door, and a rattle as the intruder attempted, as Charlie saw it, to force entry.

"Hello, anyone in there? Ms Prentiss? Charlie?"

Charlie remained silent. If she ignored him he might go away. She didn't recognize the voice. He could be anyone, though from the sound of it he was university staff. His tone was well modulated, deep, and certain. Philosophy department, maybe.

"I know you're in there, Ms Prentiss. They told me where you'd be when I called the main office. And you sent me an email a couple of minutes ago. And, to demonstrate my detection skills even further, I can smell your hot chocolate."

Charlie tiptoed over to the door and pressed her ear against it. Shit. It must be Professor Markham. English Literature. She'd just emailed him with a list of additional students for next term. He'd be mad. No way she could let him in.

"If you don't open up I'm going to fetch the porter. I need to speak with you."

He began rapping on the door again. Carefully she turned the key in the lock and swiftly pulled the door open. A tall man came stumbling in, just managing to hold on to his balance. And his dignity.

"Miss Prentiss, I presume?"

"Charlie." She shook the proffered hand. His shake was firm and warm. She glanced up at him. No half-moon glasses. No black lock of hair over a brooding brow. His long dark blond hair was tied back. University regulations, no doubt. She couldn't quite see whether his dark wool jacket was patched at the elbows, but his crisp white shirt, open at the neck, was refreshingly bow-tie free. His deep blue eyes held hers. He was in his mid-thirties maybe, tiny creases just beginning to appear round his eyes. Young to be a Professor. He must be good, she thought. And he was sexy too. She liked that in an academic.

"Evan, please. I heard you'd moved here. On your own. I've something …" His voice trailed away. Not very articulate for a professor, Charlie smiled. Their email flirtations had reached quite a fever pitch just lately. She wondered if meeting her in the flesh was the disappointment that Charlie had hoped to avoid.

"Is it about the extra students?"

"Extra students? No, it's not."

The professor appeared to be rooted to the spot, his gaze fixed on Charlie. Then he took a step forward, and another one. The circular room felt tiny now, as though the walls had closed in since the number of occupants had doubled. Charlie was certain she could feel the warmth of his breath on her cheek. She glanced around. To reach her desk she would need to step past him. But then she would be in a place of relative safety. And power.

"Excuse me, Professor." Charlie was proud of her

nimble footwork. Not bad for a girl of her generous proportions. She had almost reached her desk when she felt his arm hold hers. Not just a light touch – but a firm grasp. It felt proprietorial, a little invasive. But kind of good too. Not that she was going to let him know that. Not yet.

"I think you'll find touching university employees without their express permission is breaking the rules, Professor. One phone call and I could have you suspended within minutes."

Charlie was proud of herself. She'd managed to sound suitably self-righteous. Not easy when she wanted to encourage the man's touch rather than repel it. But she needed to feel more certain of his motives. And she wanted him to work for it a little too. Professor Markham loosened his grip on Charlie's arm, and trailed his fingers up to her hair, twisting a lock round his forefinger.

"You're not going to, are you though, Charlie. We both know that."

"You're rather sure of yourself, Professor. And, unless I've missed something, I don't believe you've declared your reasons for being here. I thought the matter of the extra students had been settled."

Charlie knew she could pull away, sit at her desk and tap away at her keyboard. Break the connection between them. Insist that she had work to do. Emails to compose. Calls to make. But she didn't. Because every tiny tug he made as he wound her hair round his finger caused her to shudder imperceptibly. She was becoming extremely aroused. Then he let go and stepped back. She held her breath. She didn't really think this wouldn't continue and progress, but she would be mighty disappointed now if he began to complain about his timetable, in time-honoured professorial fashion.

"God, you're gorgeous. I've got to see more of you."

She released her breath. Relief and desire flooded over her. She really wanted him. He was beautiful. More like Rapunzel than she would ever be. She'd rescue him, any day.

"Plenty of me to see, Professor. Where shall we begin?"

She slid her jacket from her shoulders and threw it across her chair. Her blouse was silk and form-fitting. The tiny mother of pearl buttons strained over her breasts. She met his gaze.

"Shall I, or would you prefer to …?" She allowed her voice to trail away as she plucked at the top button. He pushed her hand away.

"I think it would only be gentlemanly if I took over from here. Don't you?"

His hands were surprisingly deft. Her blouse fell open in moments. She allowed him to shrug it off her arms. Let him think he had some control. She watched him take her in. He licked his lips. An involuntary action. Then he kissed her. Gently at first. Then more insistent. His tongue pushed her lips apart, roved round her mouth, engaging with her tongue. She pushed her thighs together, enjoying the tingling sensation between her legs that accompanied the kiss. This was beginning to feel very good indeed. Blissful. She was relishing every moment. She felt his hands slide the satin straps of her bra off her shoulders. A man of many talents she thought. Kissing and undressing her in one fell swoop. He released her breasts, and undid the clasp. Charlie fought the instinct to wrap her arms around her, to hide herself. Yes she was big; her breasts fell on release, not for her the tiny, perky tits of some of her more flat-chested colleagues. But she was quite certain the Professor wasn't going to be disappointed by their fullness. And she was soon proved right, as he buried his face in her cleavage; sucking, licking, tugging on her nipples with his teeth; circling them with his tongue. And her nipples responded in the way they knew how: hardening, demonstrating her desire. She was really enjoying herself. Looking up, he took the weight of her breasts in his hands and smiled at her. Their look was complicit. Neither of them needed to speak. Their mutual pleasure was mounting. He let go of her breasts and ran his hands down her side. Her skin shone white, pearlescent in the deliberately dim light. Her waist, though it could never be called small, was at least curvy, blending perfectly into the fullness of her hips and stomach. The professor's breath was beginning to come quickly now, as tucked his fingers into the waistband of her skirt. Snug to say the least, it was a relief when his hands made it to the centre of her back, released the button and tugged down the zip. Her skirt was too tight to merely fall to the floor. He had to ease it over her hips, a task she was happy to help him with by twisting and wriggling as it moved down slowly, but surely. He gasped as her black satin suspender belt was revealed, holding up sheer black stockings. An obviously unexpected bonus, she thought. And if he was surprised she wasn't wearing knickers, he didn't show it. He gazed at her dark, well-trimmed mound, licking his lips, looking as though he wanted to devour her there and then. But he didn't. Not yet. Her skirt had left a red mark round her waist, a mark he traced round with his fingers, then planted tiny kisses on, his hands following the curve of her hips, and beginning to part her thighs. Time to stop him right there, thought Charlie.

"I think I'm at a bit of a disadvantage, Professor, don't you? Me being almost naked, you still fully clothed?"

He nodded his agreement. She unbuttoned his shirt, discarding it in the increasing pile of clothes on her chair. His chest was slim and tanned, hairless. She ran her hands over him, slowly moving down to his chinos, loosening his belt. His erection pressed through the cream cotton, and his breath came quick and fast as she let her fingertip trail down the length of his cock. She felt him flex in response to her touch. He was hard and ready. His chinos and boxers fell from him easily and she stepped back to admire his cock, erect and proud against his slim hips. Charlie grinned; they were going to fit together well. She was hungry for him now, wanted to devour him. She bent to kiss the tip of his penis, tasting the salty sweetness, circling him with her tongue, slowly, firmly. She heard him sigh. She held his balls in the palm of her hand and felt them tense. He was close to coming. Then he pulled himself out of her mouth.

"Not yet, not like that, later. I want to get deep inside you."

Charlie was all for that. They began kissing again. He reached round her, fondling her arse, before lifting her, without too much effort on his part, on to her desk, brushing a pile of paperwork to the floor. She crossed her legs as he knelt in front of her. He bent to pull off her shoes and kiss his way up her legs, gently parting them as he went and finally arriving at the point where her stockings finished and he was faced with an expanse of white flesh. He paid particular attention here, with tongue and fingers, seemingly fascinated by the tops of Charlie's thighs, as a nineteenth-century gentleman may have been about a lady's briefly glimpsed ankle. With little effort Charlie reached for his cock, using a feather light touch at first, increasing the pressure as he drew closer to her cunt. His hands were kneading her flesh.

"Fuck, Charlie, you're perfect, just how I imagined, and there's so much of you to enjoy."

"Professor, you academics do go on so; how about a little more action?" Charlie shuffled her arse to the front of the desk, willing him to bury himself deep inside her. Just the thought made her cunt tighten with need. She felt her juices trickle onto the dark wood desk. She wanted his cock to fill her, to feel him push and press into her flesh, to make her shudder with desire and satisfaction. These thoughts were interrupted by a sharp knock on the door.

"Ssh," Charlie said, unnecessarily, pressing her forefinger to her lips. There was no chance the professor was going to be bouncing up, opening the door and inviting in whoever was waiting there. Not with his tongue exploring the upper regions of her thigh, and threatening to investigate her folds any moment soon.

"Hey, Charlie, it's me, Dr Neilson. I just had a, errm, timetabling question for you."

Then there was silence. Professor Markham's tongue had begun to circle her clit, and boy did it feel sweet. She was willing him to press on, aching to feel his tongue inside her. This was exquisite. She could feel her cunt contract in readiness. And then she was certain he shook his head, telling her to ignore their unwanted guest, a movement that threatened to send her over the edge. She threw her head back and remained as still as she could, waiting for her imminent orgasm to subside to mere overwhelming desire.

"Ok, Charlie, I'll drop you an email, and maybe come back another time." Dr Neilson's footsteps faded away as he retreated down the staircase. Professor Markham pulled himself away from her cunt, and nuzzled his face into the softness of her stomach. Momentarily she was disappointed. But then her disappointment faded as he thrust his fingers into her, twisted and turned them around, as if exploring her readiness, pulled them from her and licked the juices that ran down his fingers. They held each other's gaze. He snapped one suspender against her thigh, sending a shudder through her. Then he snapped the other. Charlie felt her skin sting. Then he pushed her thighs wide apart and began to thrust his cock deep into her. And boy was she ready. And she was correct too, about how well they would fit together. His cock filled her, thrust into her, exploring her folds like they were undiscovered territory. She reached down and fingered her clit, knowing it would take little to tip her over into full-blown orgasm. He moved her hand away, and with deft fingers he rubbed her engorged nub, and thrust into her, setting a rhythm that suited them both. As he thrust deeper Charlie felt herself tighten around him, the movements involuntary, and deeply pleasurable, and moments later her orgasm washed over her, and she lost all sense of where she was, just concentrating on willing the Professor to fuck her hard. Which he did, reaching his own climax moments later, groaning as his cum filled her, and he held on to her round hips to intensify the sensation for them both.

"Christ Charlie, that was good," he moaned, pulling out of her. Kneeling, he rested his head in her lap. She stroked his hair; allowing his fingers to explore her folds again, tweaking the last gasps of her orgasm from her.

"I don't make a habit of this you know, Charlie. Ravishing beautiful, voluptuous maidens in towers."

She smiled, not minding if he did. She loved a good ravishing. And if he thought of her as a maiden, all well and good. After a few minutes he stood and dressed quickly. She knew if he didn't leave soon he'd be late for the two o'clock lecture she'd recently re-scheduled for him. Shrugging his jacket on she could see his eyes roving over her, sitting on the edge of her desk, clothed in stockings and suspenders, her legs apart, their mingled juices glistening on her cunt. She held her breasts up, offering them to him. She saw him hesitate, torn between duty and desire, and he stepped towards her, burying his head again for one last long nuzzle. Then he turned and left. Once she heard his footsteps retreat down the staircase, she dragged on her clothes, less carefully than usual. She fumbled with her blouse, quite certain that the correct button hadn't gone through the right hole. Generally she took far more care with her appearance. But for now, she would do. Who was going to see her? Pulling her tight-fitting skirt over her curves, Charlie sat at her desk and pulled her laptop towards her. She began returning an email that she'd heard ping into her inbox when she and Professor Markham had been in the middle of their fuck.

To: Dr Neilson
From: Charlie Prentiss
Subject: Re:Timetabling

Apologies for missing you today, Dr Nielson. I slipped out of my office for a moment. If you would like to call tomorrow, at 11.30, perhaps we could run through any outstanding issues you may have.

Charlie gave herself a twirl in her brand new chair. She thought she deserved it. This new office was going to work out well.

NEW!!

Ultimate Curves for gorgeous,
Sexy, lovable, ladies…

Free stories, dating
and plus-size lingerie

www.ultimatecurves.com

Check out our full lingerie range at
www.ultimatecurves.com

More great books from Xcite...

Naughty Spanking One
Twenty bottom-tingling stories to make your buttocks blush!
9781906125837 £7.99

The True Confessions of a London Spank Daddy
Memoir by Peter Jones
9781906373320 £7.99

Girl Fun One
Lesbian anthology edited by Miranda Forbes
9781906373672 £7.99

The Education of Victoria
Adventures in a Victorian finishing school
9781906373696 £7.99

Sex & Satisfaction 2
Erotic short stories edited by Miranda Forbes
9781906373726 Aug 09 £7.99

Naughty! The Xcite Guide to Sexy Fun
How To book exploring edgy, kinky sex
9781906373863 Oct 09 £9.99

For more information and great offers please visit
www.xcitebooks.com